Angie and Me

Angie and Me

Rebecca C. Jones

MACMILLAN PUBLISHING CO., INC.
New York
COLLIER MACMILLAN PUBLISHERS
London

Macmillan Publishing Co., Inc.
866 Third Avenue, New York, N.Y. 10022
Collier Macmillan Canada, Ltd.
Printed in the United States of America
10 9 8 7 6 5 4 3 2 1

Library of Congress Cataloging in Publication Data
Jones, Rebecca C.
Angie and me.
Summary: During her stay at a children's hospital
where she is treated for juvenile rheumatoid arthritis,
twelve-year-old Jenna comes to terms with her illness.
[1. Rheumatoid arthritis—Fiction. 2. Hospitals—
Fiction. 3. Physically handicapped—Fiction] I. Title.
PZ7.J72478An [Fic] 81-4367 ISBN 0-02-747980-3 AACR2

For Jones and his genes.

1

I started worrying the moment I heard Dr. Cosley wanted to talk to my parents. If I had something simple wrong with me, like strep throat or double pneumonia, he would have said, "Jenna, you have something simple wrong with you, like strep throat or double pneumonia. Now, take this medicine and you'll feel better."

But he didn't say that. He said he wanted to talk to my parents.

Alone.

Mother and Daddy went in to see Dr. Cosley late Friday afternoon, after his nurses and other patients had gone home. They stayed in his office forty-seven minutes. I timed it on the big clock in the waiting room.

For the first forty-two minutes I waited alone and sweated a gallon. Dr. Cosley must be one of those energy-saving freaks who sets his air-conditioning thermostat way up. I was sitting right next to the blower, but the backs of my thighs were still sticking to the leather seat.

At 6:12 my kid sister dashed in. Yoyo always dashes. Mother says it's because she's so athletic, but Daddy says it's because she's usually late.

"Oh, good!" Yoyo said. "You're still here. I was afraid I'd be late."

1

"You *are* late. You were supposed to be here at five-thirty."

"I know." Yoyo dropped into the chair next to mine, and I got a whiff of the YMCA gym where she'd been working out. "I was practicing my dismount. It's still pretty rough."

Yoyo's nine years old, and she's a gymnast. Mother decided we should both be gymnasts after she saw Nadia Comaneci on TV a couple of years ago. She said gymnastics would give us poise and self-discipline. Besides, the Y had an afternoon gymnastics program that would keep us busy until she got off work.

At first I thought gymnastics would be fun. I pictured myself flipping over bars and prancing across mats, just like Nadia. Maybe I'd be on TV someday, too. Then I found out about the exercises you have to do, over and over. And the sweat. Gymnastics is a very sticky sport.

Yoyo doesn't mind sweat, though, and she likes gymnastics. Coach Thompson keeps saying she could Go Places. He never said that about me. He used to yell at me something awful whenever I went near the bars. After a while he stopped yelling and just stood there, shaking his head. Daddy finally let me quit.

Mother was really mad when I quit. She said it was too late to get me in a camp and she wasn't the kind of mother who would let an eleven-year-old child (actually, I'm almost twelve) run around without supervision. But Daddy calmed her down and pointed out how much poise and self-discipline I could get at the Cedar Ridge Pool every day.

Mother wasn't crazy about counting swimming as a supervised activity, but she talked to the lifeguard and decided it would be okay as long as I promised to swim and not just hang around the pool.

That's no problem because I love to swim. I like to open my eyes under water and glide near the bottom of the pool.

Sometimes I pretend I'm a hungry mermaid looking for tuna to eat.

Since I like swimming so much, Mother said I should join the Y's swim team in the fall. But I was on the gymnastics team long enough to know how that would be. They'd have some kind of competition and I would come in last and everyone would say, "The important thing is that you got out there and tried."

No thanks. I'd rather be a plain old mermaid.

"Whew, it's hot," Yoyo said, fanning herself with a magazine. "Have you seen the doctor yet?"

"No, and would you mind blowing the air in another direction? You forgot to take a shower again."

"Sorry." But she kept right on fanning herself. "I bet you have polio," she said. "They say on TV it's coming back."

"I've had the vaccine."

"Or maybe cancer."

"Shut up, Yoyo."

"Stop calling me that. My name is Yolanda."

I don't know why Yoyo doesn't like her nickname any more. It suits her personality perfectly.

She smiled sweetly. "Maybe you're going to die."

"I said shut up."

I've thought about dying. I'd miss going to junior high in the fall, but kids would probably stand around their lockers and tell each other what a terrific person I had been. The ninth-graders might even blow up my picture to fill a whole page in the yearbook, the way they did when Sandra Martin got run over last year.

But who ever heard of someone dying of swollen knees? That's what I've got. Hot, swollen, aching knees. Sometimes they hurt so much I can barely walk. It started a couple of

3

weeks ago, and Mother said it was probably just growing pains. She said lots of kids get growing pains as they approach puberty. She said we were going to the doctor just to be on the safe side.

Mother is big on safety. I guess that's because she works at Humpty Dumpty Preschool, and they always have to make sure the little kids don't fall off a swing or swallow something funny.

Dr. Cosley opened his office door and asked me to come in. I stuck my legs straight out in front of me and pushed against the sides of the chair with my arms. It didn't hurt so bad if I stood up without bending my knees too much.

The doctor took hold of my arm and led me into his office. Mother and Daddy both stood up when we came in. They were smiling really big, as if they hadn't seen me in a long time.

"Well, Jenna," Dr. Cosley said, after everyone had sat down. "We've been able to diagnose your problem as a form of arthritis. Juvenile rheumatoid arthritis, to be exact."

"Arthritis?" I almost laughed. I'd seen enough TV commercials to know you don't die of arthritis. You just take aspirin.

But Dr. Cosley wasn't laughing. "It's important to act quickly to control the disease," he said. "As I've told your parents, there's a hospital in Columbus that's done some excellent work with juvenile rheumatology patients."

"A hospital? In Columbus? Couldn't I just take some aspirin?"

He smiled. "Why don't we leave your treatment to the specialists? Frankly, I've had very little experience with JRA. But at Franklin Children's Hospital you could have specialists, therapists, the best treatment available. If you were my daughter, I'd send you to Franklin."

One look at my parents' faces and I knew I might as well be his daughter.

"How long would I have to stay?"

"We can't be sure. It depends how quickly your body. . . ."

"How long?"

"Anywhere from two to six weeks," Daddy said.

Two to six weeks! Death I could handle, but six weeks in a hospital? Summer would be over by the time I got home.

"It's a small price to pay for being able to walk back to school in the fall," Dr. Cosley said.

I looked at the man. He was serious.

"But the people on TV have arthritis and they don't have to go to a hospital. They just take aspirin."

"This is a different kind of arthritis," he said. "The kind that strikes young people. It can be very serious."

"Are you sure that's what I've got? Mother said it was just growing pains."

She took my hand. "I was wrong," she said. I don't think I'd ever heard her say that before.

"But I don't want to go to a hospital. Not during the summer." I turned to Daddy. "I'd rather take gymnastics, even."

He smiled. "I wish you could."

"Then it's settled," Dr. Cosley said, but I wasn't feeling at all settled. "I'll call Franklin first thing in the morning, Mrs. Matthews, and I'll let you know when they can take her." He stood up, and we were dismissed.

Back in the waiting room, Yoyo said she was hungry, and how about a pizza? Then she remembered to ask what the doctor had said.

5

"We'll talk about it after supper," Daddy said.

"Pizza?" she asked again.

Daddy said okay, and for once Mother didn't say anything about empty calories. She just frowned at the floor, the same way she does when school is canceled on account of snow and she has to make other arrangements for us.

Well, she doesn't have to worry about making other arrangements for me. I'm not going to a hospital. Not for any two to six weeks, I'm not. I don't know how I'll get out of it, but I will.

2

Mother was smiling again by the time we got into the car. She started talking in her peppy nursery-school voice.

"This is going to be such fun!" she said. "We'll buy some new nighties, maybe a bathrobe. It'll be just like buying a trousseau!"

"True who?" Yoyo asked.

"Trousseau, dummy," I said. "That's what brides buy before they get married."

"Is Jenna getting married?"

Daddy laughed. "She's going to a hospital."

"Really?" Yoyo looked at me with respect. "But what's that got to do with getting married?"

Daddy sighed. "We'll talk about it after supper."

We picked up a mushroom and peperoni pizza at Sol's Pizzeria. While we ate in the kitchen, Mother talked about a kid at Humpty Dumpty who had a bad case of poison ivy. Daddy told about the time he got poison ivy at camp. I kept asking questions. I figured the more they thought about poison ivy, the less they would think about that hospital in Columbus. Maybe they'd forget all about it.

After supper Daddy helped me walk out to the living room. Yoyo came with us and turned on the TV. She even

7

ran to get my glasses for me. Then Daddy called her back to the kitchen to help clean up.

They talked so quietly that I couldn't hear what they were saying. But I knew they were talking about my legs. They wouldn't be so hush-hush about poison ivy.

After a while they all came out to the living room. Yoyo sat down and pretended to watch TV. But she kept sneaking looks at my legs.

"What's the matter?" I said finally. "Haven't you ever seen a pair of legs?"

"Not crippled legs," Yoyo said.

Mother gasped.

Daddy jumped up and yelled something at Yoyo. I didn't hear it, though. I just kept hearing that one word, over and over.

Crippled.

It sounded so permanent and ugly. Like those old ladies who hobble down the street with wrinkled, crabby faces, always worried that some kid is going to knock them over.

No wonder they wanted to put me in a hospital for the rest of the summer. Who'd want to have a crippled kid hanging around the house?

"I'm not crippled!" I shouted.

"Of course you aren't," Daddy said.

"That's a very unfortunate word," Mother said. "I have no idea where Yolanda heard it."

"You said her legs don't work right," Yoyo said. "Isn't that what crippled means?"

"My legs work fine!"

"Well, dear, you do have arthritis, and that makes your legs...."

"No, I don't!" I yelled. "I don't have arthritis!"

"Now, Jenna, Dr. Cosley said . . . ," Mother began.

8

"I don't care what he said! I don't have arthritis! I just have growing pains, that's all! And I'm going to outgrow them any day now, so you might as well forget about sticking me in a hospital!"

"I think it's important for you to be honest with yourself," Daddy said.

"I *am* being honest. My legs are beginning to feel better already. Look, I can walk just fine." I pushed myself up and took one stiff-legged step.

"Jenna . . . . " Mother sounded worried.

"No, no, let her go," Daddy said. He turned to me. "Since you're feeling so much better, would you mind going outside and turning on the sprinkler? The grass needs watering."

The front door was six steps away. Holding my breath and keeping my legs as straight as possible, I made it. I opened the door and looked out.

There, in front of me, were three concrete steps leading to the sidewalk and yard below. I'd never noticed how steep they were.

"Can you make it?" Daddy asked. He was right behind me.

"Sure." I grasped the iron railing and bent my left knee just enough to let my right leg drop to the step below. When I started to straighten my knee, I felt a hot knife slice through it. I began to fall.

Daddy caught me. He dropped to the step below, with me on his lap. He held me tight. After a few minutes he let go a little. "Look at your knees, honey," he said.

I expected to see a knife sticking out of my left one, but nothing was there. Nothing but a swollen red kneecap.

"That really must hurt," he said.

I couldn't say anything. My knees looked so red and angry. They never used to look like that. I'd never paid much

9

attention to them, in fact, unless I skinned one or wore a hole through my jeans. I wondered what had made them change.

"I'd do anything in the world to make your knees stop hurting," Daddy said. "I'm even willing to let you go away for a while."

Maybe it was all those gymnastics classes. Maybe that's what made my knees so sick. Then why didn't Yoyo get arthritis, too? Or maybe it was all that flutter kicking at the pool. But Sunny Robinson and Celia Pifer went to the pool almost every day, too, and their knees were fine. Why did mine hurt so much?

"Well?" Daddy said. "Do you want to stay like this, or do you want to get some help?"

There wasn't much choice.

"Will you and Mother come with me?"

"One of us will take you, but we can't stay in Columbus. We have our jobs and everything here to take care of. But we'll come every weekend and we'll call and we'll write lots of letters."

"Oh, boy," I muttered.

Daddy laughed. "Then it's settled."

And this time I knew it was.

He helped me up, and we went inside.

"Jenna's decided to give the hospital a chance," Daddy told Mother and Yoyo.

"That's good," said Mother. "I'm sure it's the best thing."

"Couldn't you even turn on the sprinkler, Jen?" Yoyo asked.

"We forgot about the sprinkler," Daddy said. "We sat down and had a little talk instead."

"That's okay," Yoyo said. "I can turn it on."

She opened the door and skipped down the steps.

It just wasn't fair.

10

3

The phone rang. It was Celia. She's my half best friend. Sunny is the other half. Up until last week, when my legs started to get really bad, the three of us went to the pool every day, even when it rained. Jason—that's the lifeguard —let us into the clubhouse, and he taught us to play three-man poker. Mother doesn't know about that.

"So what did the doctor say?" Celia asked.

"I've got arthritis."

"Be serious. What did he say?"

"I told you, I've got arthritis."

There was a pause.

"You can't have arthritis," she said. "My grandmother has it, and she says arthritis is the scourge of the old."

"This is a different kind of arthritis. It's called juvenile rheumatoid arthritis."

"That's a mouthful."

"The doctor calls it JRA."

"Sounds like it's part of the FBI," she said. "So what do you do about this JRA?"

"I'm going to a hospital. In Columbus."

"A hospital? In Columbus? Wow."

"They have specialists there."

"My grandmother doesn't go to a specialist."

"I told you, this is a different kind of arthritis."

"Must be. Wait till I tell Sunny."

About seven minutes later the phone rang. It was Sunny. Sunny's real name is Sandra, but she wants the kids in junior high to call her Sunny, so Celia and I are supposed to talk it up this summer.

"Tell me this is a joke," she said.

"It's no joke."

"You've got arthritis?"

"Uh-huh."

"And you're going to a hospital in Columbus?"

"Uh-huh. A children's hospital."

"Oh, Lord," Sunny said. "This is worse than I thought."

"You won't tell anyone?" I said. "About the children's hospital, I mean?"

"My lips are sealed."

I figured Sunny and Celia would be at our house first thing Saturday morning. They'd probably sit by my side and tell me how brave I was. Maybe they'd even bring me a present to cheer me up. But maybe not. They might want to rush over before the stores open.

But they didn't come Saturday morning. Or Saturday afternoon. They didn't even call.

Other people called. I don't know how so many people found out about me, but the phone kept ringing and Mother kept saying, "Yes, we just found out . . . she'll go in the hospital Monday . . . no, we don't know how long . . . we just have to wait and see . . . thank you so much . . . I'll tell her you called."

Mrs. Kozloski from next door brought a bouquet of French marigolds from her garden. The same French marigolds, she said, that keep her tomato plants from getting bugs.

Mrs. Levin, who lives on the other side of us, sent over a

banana nut bread, just like she did when Grandma Matthews died last fall.

Even Coach Thompson stopped by, with a paint-by-number set.

"I always thought there was something physically wrong with you," he said.

I wondered why Sunny and Celia didn't come. Maybe their mothers were afraid they'd catch arthritis. I called Celia to tell her I wasn't contagious, but her mother said she was at the pool.

At the pool.

"Do you know if she's coming over to my house afterward?" I asked.

"Not that I know of," Mrs. Pifer said. "She said something about going to the Flagpole for ice cream."

So. Here I am, under the scourge of arthritis, and what are Sunny and Celia doing? Splashing in pools and licking ice-cream cones, that's what. Acting like everything's normal. When it's not. Some best friends!

They came Sunday afternoon. Sunny was wearing her new bra, the one that makes her look curvy in front. Celia was probably wearing a bra, too, but I couldn't tell. She's built like me. We have to stuff tissues into our Gro-Bras if we want to look curvy.

They bounced into the room. Sunny's aunt used to be a model in Cleveland, and she once told us the prettiest girls always have a smile on their lips and an extra bounce in their step. So we started walking with a bounce. I had to stop when my legs started hurting, but Sunny and Celia still bounce.

"Oh, hi." I tried to sound a little surprised so they wouldn't think I'd been waiting around for them all weekend.

"You don't look at all sick," Celia said.

"Thanks."

"Your tan hasn't faded a bit," Sunny said, sort of wistfully.

Sunny would probably trade her blond hair and curvy front for a tan like mine. The sun turns her red until she peels, and it gives Celia a jillion freckles. I may have a flat chest and an overgrown nose, but I get a fantastic tan every summer. Mother always says I'll get skin cancer or early wrinkles. I bet she never thought of arthritis.

"Oh, you're still working on tans, aren't you?" I said, very sweetly. "I guess that's why you couldn't come over yesterday."

"Well. . . ." Celia looked uncomfortable. So did Sunny.

"It's probably a good thing you didn't come," I said. "I might not have had time to see you. Lots of people were here. Somebody even brought me flowers." I nodded toward the French marigolds on my dresser.

"Flowers!" Sunny said. "Are they from Joe Korth?"

Sunny thinks Joe Korth likes me. She's very interested in boys.

"We brought you something, too," Celia said. She nodded to Sunny, who went out to the hall to get a large paper bag. "Sorry it isn't wrapped."

Sunny pulled out a poster of a monkey holding a noose around his neck. A cartoon bubble over his head said, "Hang in there, kid."

So. They didn't just swim and eat ice-cream cones yesterday. They also thought about me.

"Do you like it?" Celia asked.

"It's perfect," I said. "Just perfect."

"What's that?" Mother asked when I slipped the rolled-up poster into the suitcase she was packing.

"Oh, it's just something Sunny and Celia gave me."

"May I see it?"

Reluctantly, I unrolled the picture of the monkey in a noose. Mother stared at it.

"Hey, that's neat!" Yoyo said. "Look at the way his tongue hangs out."

Mother still didn't say anything. I started to roll up the poster.

"Jenna."

"Yes, Mother?"

"I can't let you take that poster with you."

"Why not?"

"It's not very . . . tasteful."

"But I like it."

Mother took the poster. "I'm sorry, honey. But I don't want you to get off on the wrong foot with the hospital staff." She set the poster on my bed, and Yoyo unrolled it to take another look.

"But look," Mother said brightly, "I bought your trousseau yesterday afternoon." She pulled three new nightgowns and one new bathrobe out of a shopping bag. "Do you like them?"

"They're very pretty," I said. "But couldn't I take the poster with me if I promise to put it where no one will see it?"

"The nightgowns were on sale, so I got a really good price," Mother said. "I should have gotten some for Yolanda, but I didn't think of it."

"I could keep it in my suitcase and never take it out," I said.

"I just hope they let you wear them," she said.

"Huh?"

"I said I hope they let you wear your new nightgowns."

"Why wouldn't they?"

"Sometimes hospitals want patients to wear special gowns that tie in the back."

"Why?"

"I'm not sure. Maybe they're easier to put on and take off. Or maybe they don't get in the way of special treatments."

I wondered what kind of special treatments I'd get. Would they hurt?

I looked at the poster on the bed. It looked as if the monkey was pulling the noose tighter.

4

"Jenna Matthews."

"At last," Mother said. We'd been sitting in the hospital lobby for almost an hour. I was willing to wait another hour—or even a week—but Mother kept looking at her watch and saying she hoped she'd have time to meet my doctor.

Mother helped me walk over to a central desk where a beak-nosed old nurse sat.

"Welcome to Franklin." Beak Nose crinkled up her face into a smile that made her look like the Wicked Witch of the West getting ready to cackle. She fastened a turquoise plastic bracelet around my left wrist. My name and a string of numbers were typed on it. Then Beak Nose pointed me toward a wheelchair. "Sit down, dear, so you can go for a little ride," she said.

Mother guided me toward the chair.

"Pink Lady!" Beak Nose called out, and, sure enough, a gray-haired lady wearing a hot-pink uniform appeared. "Take this patient to Three North," Beak Nose said as she handed the Pink Lady a manila folder with my name on it.

"All righty!" the Pink Lady sang. She smiled at me. "My, what a pretty tan!"

"Thanks," I said. "I hope I don't lose it here."

"I'm sure the doctors will fix you up so you'll be back outside in no time," she said, pushing my wheelchair toward a set of elevators. Mother started to follow us, but Beak Nose called her back to fill out some papers.

The elevator was huge, and when it stopped on the second floor, I saw why. An orderly pushed a long stretcher onto the elevator, and it fit perfectly.

A kid on the stretcher had some tubes stuck in his mouth, and every time he breathed, it sounded like he was sucking the last bit of soda out of a straw. I was glad to get off on the third floor.

"Have you ever been in a hospital before, uh, Jenna?" The Pink Lady sneaked a look at my manila folder before she tagged my name onto her question.

"No."

"Well, I'm sure you'll like it here." She sprinkled sugar over her words, the way Mother does when she talks to her preschoolers. "You'll make lots of new friends. Children come here from all over the state, you know."

"You make it sound like a resort."

The Pink Lady laughed. "I like a child with a sense of humor," she said. "I really do."

A bathrobed boy, about the size of a Muppet, grinned at me as he struggled down the hall on crutches. A little girl, propped in a sunny corner of her room, waved as we passed her door. In another room, a toddler clutched the bars of his crib and cried for Mama.

The place looked like a Kiddieland for Sickies.

"Here we are." The Pink Lady stopped the wheelchair in front of a high horseshoe-shaped desk in the middle of the corridor. A fleshy face, wearing a white nurse's cap and a creased frown, peered over the counter at me.

"This is Mrs. Anderson, the head nurse," said the Pink Lady. "She'll take care of you now."

When Mrs. Anderson came around the desk to inspect me more closely, I gulped. I'd never seen such an enormous woman. Her breasts were about the size of basketballs.

"Your mother is still in admissions, but we'll take you to your room now." Her voice had none of the Pink Lady's sugar coating. "Jim!"

A tall young man in white appeared at her command. "Jim, take Jenna to Three Forty-eight."

"Yes, ma'am!" Jim clicked his heels together, and for a moment I thought he was going to salute. But he just took charge of my wheelchair and spun it around.

We whizzed down the hall so fast that I couldn't find—let alone read—the room numbers. Just as we were about to crash through the double glass doors at the end of the corridor, Jim braked himself, and we skidded to a stop in front of the last door on the left.

He spun the wheelchair around again, and, pushing the door open with his rear, backed into the room.

"Angie, Angie, Angie," he said. "You know what Anderson thinks of closed doors." He talked through his nose to imitate his boss. "All doors must be kept open unless a patient is seeing a doctor."

"You can tell Anderson my doctor was here, but she slipped out the window."

I tried to turn around, but all I could see was Jim's white uniform. Finally he maneuvered me past a bed and turned my chair around.

"Thank God," Angie said when she saw me. "I was afraid they'd send me another second-grader."

Jim laughed. "Jenna, this is Angie Salvadore."

If Mrs. Anderson was the most enormous female I'd ever

met, Angie Salvadore had to be the skinniest. She sat on the edge of the bed, with two broomstick legs hanging from a baggy bathrobe.

"How old are you, anyway?" she asked.

"I'll be twelve in September."

"I'm already twelve," she said, but she didn't sound conceited about it. "What's wrong with you?"

"Arthritis."

"No kidding. I've never had a roommate with arthritis. Does it hurt much?"

I shrugged. I didn't want to sound like a complainer.

"I have funny blood, myself," she said.

"I'll leave you two old ladies here to discuss your ailments," Jim said. "Your mom will be here pretty soon, Jenna. In the meantime, make yourself at home." He left, and I noticed he closed the door behind him.

I looked around the room. It was easy to see which side was mine. Angie's bed was cluttered with books, magazines, and half-finished craft projects. A wreath of get-well cards was taped to the wall over her bed.

The other bed was empty, and its sheets were stretched tight. It seemed higher than Angie's, and it had tall metal bars around the head. I must have stared at those bars pretty hard because Angie said, "Don't worry, they come down."

"Actually, these beds are kind of fun," she said. "Look." She picked up a box of push buttons near her pillow and began demonstrating the possibilities. First she raised the head, then the foot of her bed. She sat in the middle of a mattress forming a wide V.

Another button controlled a TV on the wall opposite our beds. Another turned on and off a fluorescent reading lamp over her pillow. The last button—a bright red one—was marked CALL in letters big enough for me to read without my glasses. When Angie pushed it, Mrs. Anderson's voice boomed through a wall speaker between us. "Yes?"

"Oh, did I press that button?" Angie faked surprise. "I'm *so* sorry," she told the speaker.

She showed me how to use the narrow tables that swung over our beds.

"You crank them up and down," she said, "and if you lift the top, there's a mirror and a secret hiding place."

"What do you mean, secret?" I asked. "Doesn't everyone know it's there?"

"*You* didn't, did you?"

She continued her tour of the facilities, pointing out my locker, our joint dresser, and the bathroom door. She gestured with a hand so thin that I could almost see right through it. I wondered what kind of funny blood could cause such skinniness.

"You've got the bathroom bed now, but after I leave, you can move over to the window bed," she said. "You can look across the courtyard and see right into other kids' windows."

"After you leave?" I said. "Are you going home soon?"

"Oh, I don't know. I've been coming and going for a couple of years now. I usually stay about a month."

"My doctor said I'd be here two to six weeks," I said.

Angie nodded. "They wouldn't put you here unless they expected you to be staying a month or so."

I looked around the room again. I sure didn't want to stay a month. That would be one third of the summer, one twelfth of the year, one big chunk of my life. I'd lose my tan for sure.

"Do we have to stay in this room all the time?" I asked.

"Oh, no," Angie said. "That is, it depends on your doctor. Mine lets me walk around to other rooms."

I looked at her broomstick legs. They didn't look like· they'd make it to the bathroom, let alone down the hall.

"I use that walker over there." She pointed to a four-legged metal contraption at the end of her bed. "Maybe they'll give you one, too."

That's all I need to turn myself into a full-fledged cripple.

The door opened, and in came Mother, struggling with my suitcase.

"I thought I'd never find you!" She dropped the suitcase on a chair and pushed herself up onto the empty bed. "I took the wrong elevator, and when I got out, I found I was on Three *South,* so I . . . ." Mother's mouth stopped when her eyes fell on Angie. She gave me a meaningful look, and I introduced them.

"Are your parents here, Angie?" Mother asked.

"No, we live in Piqua, and they can only come on weekends."

Mother nodded. "That's the way it is with us. I'm the program director at a preschool center, and I can't normally get away during the week." Mother likes to tell people about her job right off the bat. I think she's afraid people will peg her as a housewife.

"What's a preschool center?" Angie asked. "Is that the same thing as a day-care center?"

"Goodness, no," Mother said proudly. "We stress cognitive learning, even in the summer."

"My parents run a shoe store," Angie said. "They hired a high school kid to work in the store on Saturdays so my mother can come here. The store is closed on Sundays, so they both come."

As soon as she said her parents ran a shoe store, I couldn't help looking at her feet. She wore big pink balls of fur, the kind Mother never lets us buy because she says they get matty and don't wash well. Angie's weren't matty, though. She probably gets new shoes all the time, just like we get extra copies of the newspaper because Daddy is city editor.

The door swung open. "Angela, how many times have I told you to keep your door open? And those cards! You know it's against hospital rules to tape anything on the walls." It was Mrs. Anderson.

"Mrs. Matthews, I have more papers for you to . . . ." She stopped when she saw Mother. Her chest swelled up until the basketball breasts looked like they were ready to pop off. "Mrs. Matthews, visitors are not allowed to sit on the patients' beds!"

"Oh, I'm sorry." Mother slipped off the bed and stood at attention, just as Jim had, while Mrs. Anderson instructed her about the signing of the papers.

After the nurse left, Angie said, "Don't worry about Anderson. She comes on that way with everyone."

"I'll have to remember we aren't at home anymore," Mother said. "Things are different here."

That's for sure. I could hear a kid somewhere down the hall, crying for Mama.

Mother put on her nursery school voice and said it was time to Go Exploring. She pushed me down the hall to the nurses' station. We turned left and went all the way down another big hall. We must have passed a hundred kids, maybe more. All of them sick.

At the end of the hall was a huge room with big windows along one wall.

"Oh, the sunroom," Mother said. "How nice."

But it wasn't very sunny. All you could see out the windows was the brick wall of another wing of the hospital. Somebody was evidently trying to save on electricity, too, because none of the overhead lights was on. In the grayness, a couple of little kids argued over a wobbly wagon, another kid was wandering around in dirty diapers, and a nurse shouted for Jason to come take his medicine.

I didn't like it, not at all.

"Mother, do I have to stay here?"

"Of course not. Let's go back to your room."

"No, I mean, can't I go home with you?" I thought of Daddy, and even Yoyo, lovingly.

Mother pulled up a kindergarten-sized chair and sat down. "You want to get better, don't you?"

I looked around the room. I wasn't sure.

She tried again. "You want to walk, don't you?"

"I can walk now."

"Of course you can," Mother said, the same way she agrees with four-year-olds who think they can fly.

I looked at my swollen knees. There wasn't anything else to say.

Mother stood up. "Let's go back to your room. I don't want to miss the doctor when he comes."

When we got back to the room, a woman with a tray full of needles and glass tubes was waiting for me. Angie introduced her as her friend the Vampire, and they both laughed.

The Vampire told me to hold out my arm. She tied a plastic tube just above my elbow and began poking around for blood vessels in the crook of my arm.

"How do you think I got so thin?" Angie asked. "The Vampire drained all my blood out of me."

"Really?" I pictured myself sitting by the pool, with broomstick legs hanging out of a baggy bathing suit.

"Oh, Angie, you're such a tease!" The Vampire laughed and jabbed my arm.

24

5

Mother refused to go out for lunch. She said she knew the doctor would come the minute she stepped out of the room. She was right. She went to the bathroom, and Dr. Boggs arrived.

He didn't come alone. He led in a small army of men and women dressed in white uniforms. One of them pulled a curtain separating me from Angie. The others lined up around my wheelchair while Dr. Boggs studied my manila folder.

We all heard the toilet flush. Mother came out and shook hands with Dr. Boggs. That's when I noticed how short he was. He barely came up to her shoulders.

"I hope you don't mind these students assisting in the examination of your daughter," Dr. Boggs said.

"Of course not," Mother said. "I work with students myself."

"Good." Dr. Boggs turned to the student army. "The home physician has made a diagnosis of JRA," he said. Everyone looked me over with bug eyes that reminded me of Yoyo.

He began bending and pressing my joints. My elbows and wrists hurt a little, but I could stand it. When he got to my legs, though, I told him he'd better stop.

"Why?" he asked, smiling.

"Because my knees hurt, really bad."

"I'll try to be careful."

But he wasn't. He bent them until they hurt so bad that I wanted to scream. But I didn't. Not with all those people there. After he worked me over, he stepped back a few feet. "Can you walk this far by yourself?" he asked.

One of the students helped me up, and the others moved back. I wished they'd leave the room or look out the window, but they all just stared at me, waiting to see how I walked. A couple even crouched on the floor to get a better view of my legs.

I walked kind of stiff-legged, trying not to bend my knees too much.

"Very good," said Dr. Boggs. He took my hand and guided me back to the wheelchair. Then he turned to the troops. "What would you tell this patient on her first day at Franklin?"

"Don't cross Mrs. Anderson," one voice said, and the others laughed.

Dr. Boggs smiled. "Other than that?"

"I presume the patient is scheduled for a program of medication, therapy, and exercise?" a young woman asked. Dr. Boggs nodded.

"In that case," she said, "I would remind her of the importance of avoiding falls that could injure her joints. She should use a wheelchair for long distances and a walker for just moving about the room."

"Anything else?" Dr. Boggs asked.

"Rest is extremely important in the treatment of arthritis," the woman answered. "She should not overtire herself, and she should schedule regular rest periods during the day, in addition to an early bedtime at night."

"If you follow that advice, Jenna, you should do just fine."

Dr. Boggs smiled again and nodded toward the door, signaling his troops to retreat.

"Just a minute, Doctor," Mother said. "I have a few questions."

The doctor stopped. "Yes?"

Mother was standing at attention again, just like she had for Mrs. Anderson. "Well, I, uh . . . ."

Dr. Boggs patted her shoulder. "I'm sure you have many questions, Mrs. Matthews. Write them down before our next visit, and we'll discuss them."

"But . . . . " Mother was left with her mouth open. Dr. Boggs turned, and the troop opened its ranks for him to pass through. Evidently he had to lead the march into the next room.

After they were gone, Mother pulled back the curtain so we could see Angie again. "Is it always this rushed?" she asked.

"Depends on the doctor," Angie said. "Mine comes in by herself and takes all the time in the world."

"Maybe I should change illnesses," I said. Mother looked puzzled. "Then I could change doctors." I always have to explain jokes to her.

Mother helped me change into my new pink nightgown and bathrobe. Then she looked at her watch. I knew what was coming next.

"If I want to get home before dark, I'd better leave now. You'll be all right here."

"Sure I will." My voice sounded funny.

"I wish I could stay with you. But . . . ." Her voice sounded funny, too.

"I know. Daddy already explained."

She hugged me real hard. Then she was gone.

"Hey, Jenna." Even before I saw him, I heard Jim. "I

brought you a deluxe model." He held up a walker, just like Angie's. "Can you show her how to use it, Angie?"

She got out of bed and positioned herself so the metal bars surrounded her on three sides. She gripped the bars and shuffled forward, very slowly.

She looked like a little old lady, so skinny and bent over her walker like that. Her dark brown hair was matted flat in the back, where her head had been against the pillow.

"Now you try it," Jim said, sliding a walker to me.

I stood up straight and fluffed my hair in the back so I wouldn't look like Angie. But I shuffled just as slowly. I thought of Yoyo, probably flipping her body over the bars at the YMCA at that very moment.

"Hey, you learn real fast!" Jim smiled, but I didn't smile back. "Remember, you're supposed to use this thing whenever you're walking around, just to make sure you don't fall."

As soon as he was gone, I pushed the walker over to a chair by the TV and sat down. If I have to be crippled, at least I'll do it with dignity. I'm not about to start pushing some dumb contraption around just to hold me up.

"If you don't like the walker, I guess you could use the wheelchair," Angie said.

The wheelchair, with its leather seat and big steel wheels, grinned at me.

"No," I said. "I'll just stay here."

Angie didn't seem to hear. "In fact, I bet we could both use your wheelchair."

"Huh?"

She shuffled over and gripped the chair's handles. "I can use this just like a walker," she said. She took a couple of steps with it, then turned to me. "I feel pretty dumb, pushing an empty wheelchair. Want to go for a ride?"

"No, I think I'll just stay here for a while."

"Please? I don't want to have to use my walker."

I could understand that. "Where would we go?"

"I'll take you around to meet some other kids."

"Well, okay." I sat in the wheelchair.

Angie dragged one foot after another. If we'd moved any slower, we would have been going backward. Finally we made it to the room next door, and Angie introduced me to a girl whose chin was propped up by a stiff white cast.

"Wendy's been here for ages," Angie said. "She was in a car wreck, and her legs are paralyzed. She's had two operations so far, and she needs at least two more."

I looked on Wendy with pity. Then she opened her mouth.

"Good Lord," she said, looking at my legs. "What happened to you?"

"I've got arthritis."

"Thank God my legs *look* normal." She lifted the hem of her nightgown so I could see a pair of normal-looking knees. "I couldn't stand it if they were swollen up like yours."

A real nice kid, this Wendy.

"I bet you're wondering why I'm in a private room," she said.

Actually, I was wondering how to turn the wheelchair around and get out of there.

"A private room costs a lot more, you know, because regular insurance doesn't pay for it. But my parents are suing the jerk who did this to me, and he's going to pay for everything. I'll get millions."

"When you're rich, will you still remember your old friends at Franklin?" Angie asked, with an almost straight face.

"Of course. I'll send you all presents." Wendy smiled generously. "It's a shame you don't get money for blood diseases and arthritis."

Angie nodded. "A real pity. Right now, though, I think I'll take Jenna over to meet another poor kid. Bill isn't getting any money for being sick, either."

Wendy looked at me. "You're not going over to see Bill, looking like that, are you?"

I patted my hair. "What's wrong?"

"Do you want a *boy* to see your legs?"

I pulled the bathrobe down over my knees. Wendy handed me a red afghan from her bed. "You can use this," she said, "if you promise not to get it dirty."

For a moment I thought about throwing her lousy afghan back at her, but then I looked at my swollen knees.

"Thanks," I mumbled.

Once we were out in the hall, Angie said, "Don't let Wendy bother you. She just comes on that way because she doesn't want people to feel sorry for her."

"It works," I said.

Bill was sitting in the middle of his bed, shooting a basketball into a big metal wastebasket next to the window. His roommate, a little kid with white bandages wrapped around his head, sat next to the wastebasket to scoop out the ball and throw it back to Bill.

"Have they found out what's wrong with you yet?" Angie asked Bill.

"Nope. Dad thinks it's just growing pains, and he says it's pretty silly for me to be here." He shot another ball into the basket.

I know all about growing pains. "What hurts?" I asked.

"My leg."

"It's probably arthritis. That's what I've got."

30

He looked at the afghan covering my legs. "Does arthritis make you feel cold or something?"

"Not particularly. What I mean is . . . ."

"I think it's awful hot in here." He stretched his arms, and I could see two wet spots in the armpits of his pajamas. He looked very mature.

"Can you race that thing yet?" he asked.

"What thing?"

"Your wheelchair."

"Huh?"

"C'mon, I'll show you." He swung himself out of bed and plopped into a waiting wheelchair. "Take me out to the hall, Sam."

The kid with the bandaged head started pushing his chair. They stopped by Wendy's door and asked her if she wanted to race. She wheeled herself out.

Angie pushed me out to the hall and stopped. "You can't race with me hanging on," she said.

"I can't race, no matter what," I said. "I don't know how to work this thing."

"Now's a good time to learn."

"But what will you do?"

"I'll watch."

"I'll stay with you."

"Don't be dumb."

I gripped the wheels at my side and pushed the chair over to Wendy and Bill, who were lined up on a crack in the linoleum. Sam stood by another crack, near the glass doors, to determine the winner.

"Ready, set, go!" Angie yelled.

I pushed off, but I didn't seem to be moving very fast. The others zipped by me. Bill was a sure winner, going full speed toward the finish line. But he didn't stop, and he crashed into the double glass doors at the end of the hall. I shut my eyes when I heard the thud and waited for the sound of shattering glass. It didn't come.

Cautiously, I opened one eye.

"Man, those doors are strong," Bill said.

"Are you okay?" Sam asked.

"Sure."

I turned around and saw Angie slumped on the floor.

"Angie!" I yelled. She didn't move.

"She passed out," Wendy said matter-of-factly. "She does it all the time."

"What do we do now?" I asked.

"Nothing." Wendy nodded toward a nurse's aid who was galloping down the corridor. The aide called Jim, who picked Angie up and carried her back to our room.

6

After supper I asked Angie what it feels like to pass out.

"Nothing special," she said. "Everything goes black."

"Is it scary?"

"No. In fact, sometimes it's kind of fun. Lots of times I can still hear what's going on, and people say things they wouldn't want me to hear."

"I'll remember that. I won't talk about you while you're out."

"You better not."

A nurse rushed into the room.

"Oh, Angie!" she cried. "I almost forgot!"

She swept everything off Angie's night table and covered it with a small white cloth. She pulled two candles and a wooden cross out of a drawer and plopped them on the table.

We heard a little bell outside the door, and the student nurse stepped back. A priest walked into the room with a short-veiled nun right behind him.

"The body of Christ," said the priest.

"Amen," Angie answered. She held out her cupped hands, and the priest gave her a small white circle. She put it in her mouth and closed her eyes.

Even after he was gone, Angie kept her eyes closed. I

figured she was praying and maybe I should pray, too, just to be respectful.

Please make my legs work right again and please get me out of this hospital. Thank you.

I opened my eyes and saw that Angie was still praying, so I tried again.

And please make sure You do it all by the middle of August.

I wanted to have a couple of weeks at the pool before school started.

Amen.

Angie's eyes were open, and she was looking at me. "Do you always pray when other people get Communion?" she asked.

I didn't know what to say.

"It's okay with me," she said. "I just wondered."

"How often do you get Communion?" I asked.

"Every night."

"You must be very religious."

"I'm not sure. The main reason I get Communion so often is that the priest keeps coming."

"Are you through praying now?" I asked. "I mean, is it okay if I turn on the TV?"

"Sure."

I pressed the remote-control button and reached into my secret hiding place for my glasses.

"I didn't know you wore glasses," Angie said. "Why don't you wear them all the time?"

"Uh . . . they pinch my ears."

"Oh. I thought maybe you were just vain about them."

"Vain? Me?" I laughed a little louder than I meant to.

"You look nice in glasses."

I've heard that before, mainly from Mother.

"Glasses make you look distinctive," she said. "Without them, you look like every other girl with brown hair and a big nose."

I just stared at her.

"Oh, don't get mad," she said. "I'm no beauty either. In fact, people would consider me pretty ordinary if I didn't know how to squirt water."

"Squirt water?"

"Watch." She took a swig of water from the glass beside her bed and swished it around inside her mouth. Then she formed a toothy grin and squirted water from the gap between her teeth. When she was done, she wiped her mouth.

"Did you notice how I squirted the water in a nice round arc?" she asked. "I used to spray everywhere, but I've been practicing since I came to the hospital. I'm getting pretty good."

"You have nice control," I said.

"Can you do anything special? Like wiggle your ears, maybe?"

I thought about it. "I can touch my nose with my tongue."

"Show me."

It was the first time my tongue had performed for anyone but Yoyo, so it felt a little awkward.

"That's pretty good," Angie said.

"My tongue is very stretchy," I explained.

"Don't kid yourself. The only reason you can do that is you have a big nose."

"Well, the only reason you can squirt water is that you have a space between your front teeth."

"I know. Aren't I lucky?"

A nurse with frizzy white hair wheeled in a cart full of stuff that looked like it belonged in Yoyo's gym.

35

"Good evening, Jenna," the nurse said. I started to take off my glasses, but I decided not to. "My name is Mrs. Ruth, and I'm the evening nurse. I want you to feel free to call me if you need anything."

"Thank you," I said, with my eyes on her cart. There were several white towels, a couple of long skinny things that looked like bean-bags, and a big wooden block.

"Don't worry about these things," Mrs. Ruth said. "They're going to help keep your joints straight while you sleep."

She started to unpack the equipment but stopped.

"Would either of you like a back rub tonight?" she asked.

"I thought you'd never ask." Angie sat up and slipped off her pajama top. Maybe it was because of her skinniness, but she looked even flatter than me. I didn't feel too embarrassed when my turn came.

Mrs. Ruth squirted some nice-smelling lotion on my back. Her fingers moved rhythmically up and down my spine. I forgot about the equipment.

But Mrs. Ruth didn't forget. After my nightgown was buttoned, she told me to lie flat on my back while she tucked folded towels along my arms, wrists, and ankles. She placed long skinny sandbags along my legs, and she put the wooden block against the bottoms of my feet.

I couldn't move.

"And one more thing, Jenna," she said. "Try to keep your hands with the palms facing upward."

"How long do I have to stay like this?"

"This is your sleeping position. Try to stay like this as long as possible. If it becomes too uncomfortable in the middle of the night, let me know." She placed the call button near my right hand.

"It's too uncomfortable right now," I said.

She sighed. "This sleep position is part of your treatment.

36

It will keep your joints from becoming crooked. Besides," she added, "you'll get used to it after a couple of nights."

That was easy for her to say. She could go home and curl up in any old position she liked.

"Good night, girls," She flipped a wall switch that turned off both the TV and the lights. Some light still came in from the hall, but the room seemed to be getting darker and smaller every minute. I wanted to lift my knees, turn on my side, do anything — no matter how much it hurt. But I was trapped.

"That doesn't look very comfortable," Angie said.

"It's not."

"I wonder how they expect you to get all that rest they were talking about."

I couldn't answer. A lump was growing in my throat, and it felt like it would burst out of my ears. Mother had said they'd come see me Saturday. Maybe they would see how miserable I was, and maybe they'd take me home. Maybe. A pretty big maybe.

"Do you want to talk?" Angie asked.

She probably thought I was going to start blubbering.

"I always hate the first night in a hospital," she said. "I miss everyone at home, and I'm afraid I'll be here forever. Do you know what I mean?"

I still couldn't answer.

I never meant to go to sleep, but I must have. I saw Yoyo in the center of a crowded arena, doing her routine on the bars. She was going fast—too fast, I thought. Everyone was cheering, and she went even faster. I tried to stand up, to tell her to stop.

But I couldn't move.

7

The woman who brought in breakfast noticed my tan. She said it made me look very healthy.

"Thanks," I said. "It's beginning to fade, though."

And it was. My strap marks didn't look as white as they used to. If I didn't get out in the sun soon, I'd lose it for sure.

"Do those windows open?" I asked Angie.

"No, and it's a good thing. The fall would probably kill you."

"What are you talking about?"

"Escape, of course," she said. "I tried snitching bed sheets once so I could tie them together and let myself down that way. But the maids kept pretty close count of the sheets, and I never got enough."

I pictured Angie running away. A fugitive from medicine.

"That's pretty funny," I said. "When did all this happen?"

"A couple of years ago, the first time I came here."

"Well, I wasn't thinking of escape. I just wanted to open the window so I could sit in the sun."

She looked at me. "Why in the world would you want to do that?"

"To work on my tan."

"Is that how you got it? Sitting by an open window?"

"Of course not. I got it at a swimming pool. But I'm going to lose it here."

"That would be tragic." But she didn't sound sympathetic. I don't think she understood.

As it turned out, I didn't have much time for sitting in the sun anyway. Right after breakfast, Jim wheeled me down to a big room with exercise bars, padded tables, and tumbling mats.

"Oh, boy, have I got plans for you," a big guy said, rubbing his hands together. "My name is Ross, and I'm going to work your tail off."

"There's not much I can do," I said. The guy evidently didn't know about my legs.

"Oh, no?" He threw back his head and laughed. "We'll just see about that! But first, how about a nice warm bath?"

Unbuttoning the top half of my nightgown for Mrs. Ruth was one thing, but stripping and jumping into a tub with this big lug around was something else. I shook my head and tucked Wendy's afghan around my legs more securely.

But he didn't pay any attention. "Toni!" he called. "Our first customer is here!"

A side door opened, and a blond woman appeared. She smiled real big and showed a mouthful of braces. I had never seen a grownup with braces on her teeth before.

"You must be Jenna," she said. "We've been expecting you."

She took charge of my wheelchair and headed toward a back room. All the time she kept talking, asking me what grade I was in, how many brothers and sisters I had, and all the other stuff grownups like to know.

We went back to a little room with a big steel tub full of swirling water. Toni helped me stand up and change into a blue hospital gown that tied in the back. She was very gentle and tried not to make me bend anything. She kept asking if anything hurt.

Then she helped me get into the tub and sit down. The swirling water was warm, and my knees felt like they were floating with it.

"This is called a whirlpool," Toni said. "How does it feel?"

"Great," I said. "I wish we had one of these at home."

"You can buy a little motor that will make the water in your bathtub do the same thing."

"I'll ask my parents about it."

"Dr. Boggs will probably ask for you. And his recommendation carries a lot more weight."

Toni sure understood my parents. I liked her.

"Swimming in a heated pool would also be good for you," she said. "Is there one near your home?"

I told her about the Y's indoor pool.

"That would be perfect," she said.

I could have stayed in that whirlpool all day, but Toni said another kid was waiting to use it. She promised I could come back tomorrow. My knees felt warm and almost good.

Ross ruined that, though. He was waiting for me in the big room.

"Let's get started," he said, rubbing his hands together. He lifted me up onto a padded table and told me about a "simple little knee exercise" he wanted me to try.

"I can't do it," I said.

"How do you know? You haven't even tried."

"It'll hurt."

"Let's try it," he said, taking hold of my right leg.

"Leave my legs alone!"

He dropped my leg and just stood there a moment, shaking his head the way Coach Thompson used to.

"Okay, Jenna," he finally said. "But before you leave, I want to show you something."

He went over to a metal desk in the corner of the room. He opened the bottom drawer and pulled out a couple of books.

"I'd like to show you some pictures," he said, flipping open one of the books and handing it to me.

I saw a picture of a hand that looked like it had golf balls stuck under the knuckles. Then he turned some pages to a picture of a crooked leg with lumpy knees and ankles.

"That's what you could look like in a few years," Ross said.

I swallowed hard.

"But it doesn't have to be like this. If you take care of yourself and do the proper exercises, you can probably avoid this. It's up to you."

I didn't want to look at those sickening pictures anymore, but my eyes wouldn't move.

"It won't be easy," Ross said. "We'll try not to do any exercises that cause you real pain. But you will have to work."

My eyes finally moved, down to my swollen knees.

"Why did this have to happen to me?"

"I don't know," he said. "But the question now is, what are you going to do about it? Are you going to fight, or are you just going to give up?"

I looked at the pictures again.

"I guess I'll fight."

Ross smiled and lifted my right knee, very gently.

After lunch Jim said we were going down to the Shoe Box.

49

I tucked Wendy's afghan around my feet. I didn't want anyone staring at my swollen ankles.

But the Shoe Box has nothing to do with the feet. It's a big room with long tables and large easels. It's a lot like the arts and crafts cabin at camp, except that everyone wears a bathrobe or a hospital gown. Everyone, that is, but a couple of women running around in blue smocks.

One of the women smiled and waved when we came in. "You must be Jenna," she said. "My name is Dolores Shoemaker, but you can call me Shoe."

I rolled that one over in my head. It's not easy to call a grown woman with gray hair a silly name like Shoe.

Shoe said she'd help me "limber up" my fingers. She wheeled me over to a table and showed me how to make an octopus doll out of yarn. She said I could take some yarn back to my room and make more dolls while I watched TV.

"The more you make, the better it is for your fingers," she said. "I know a girl who's made an octopus a day for two years now. She even makes them on weekends."

"Two years! Why won't the doctors let her go home?"

Shoe laughed. "Oh, she isn't in the hospital anymore! She makes the dolls at home and sells them to a little boutique."

I thought of the millions I could make and began winding yarn.

When I got back to our room, Angie and Wendy were watching a soap opera. Someone named Marlene was telling someone named Peter that she couldn't marry him because she was going to have Dennis's child.

"But Dennis is dead," Peter said.

"His life is within me," said Marlene, her eyes downcast.

The organ music rolled, and a lady selling toilet bowl cleaner appeared on the tube.

"I don't get it," Angie said. "Dennis has been dead at least six months. If Marlene is pregnant with his kid, how come she's not fat?"

"Don't ask me," Wendy said. "You're the one who wants to watch this trash. I'd rather watch a game show any day."

"Then why don't you?" I asked. "Don't you have a TV in your room?"

Wendy gave me a hard look, but she didn't say anything.

Angie changed the subject. "Where have you been, Jenna?"

"A place called the Shoe Box. And you'll never guess what it is."

"It's occupational therapy," said Wendy. "A woman named Shoe hands you a line about selling yarn dolls to boutiques."

"How did you know?"

"I used to go there. But I convinced my parents it was a waste of time, and they told the hospital not to make me go there anymore."

"I kind of liked it."

"Really?" Wendy arched her left eyebrow. "I suppose some people do enjoy busy work."

When the doctors take Wendy's cast off, I bet her chin will still be stuck in the air.

8

The thing about hospitals is that everyone thinks they're making you do things for your own good.

I have to have shots every day. And not the decent kind of shot where you roll up your sleeve and look the other way. No, I have to get into bed and curl up on my side so my rump sticks out. Then I get stabbed.

The nurses say rear-end shots don't hurt as much. A lot they know. They just like having a wide target.

Another crummy thing nurses do is they come in every day and ask when your last bowel movement was. They mark it down on a chart and probably talk about it later.

I was in the john Tuesday night doing a number two when Mrs. Ruth knocked on the door. She said she wanted something out of the bathroom, but she would wait for me to finish.

When I was done, she went into the bathroom and took a whiff. "Phew!" she said. "I guess I can mark you down for a bowel movement today, can't I?"

I couldn't even look at Angie.

Even the volunteers get into the act of doing things for your own good. A candy striper came in Wednesday morning with a big grin on her face.

"How are we all today?" She looked a year or so older than

44

us, but she talked like a grandmother visiting Romper Room for the first time.

Angie and I told her we were all okay.

She smiled real big and looked straight at me. "What would you like to talk about today?"

"Uh, well . . . ."

"I'd like to talk about the Penny Press," Angie said.

"The Penny Press?" the candy striper said.

"You know, the newspapers that sold for a penny back in the 1830s."

"Oh, *that* Penny Press."

"Do you think they were too sensationalistic?"

"Uh, well . . . . "

"What do you think of the way they covered the Mexican War?"

"Well, actually . . . ." The candy striper examined a speck on the ceiling. Pretty soon she left.

"Why are you so interested in the Penny Press?" I asked Angie.

"I'm not. Last week we talked about Lincoln's decision to fire General Meade."

"Huh?"

"Someday she'll learn not to ask what people want to talk about. In the meantime, I'm going to keep finding new topics for her."

"You're mean, Angie, you really are."

"Nope. Just tired of do-gooders." She took a swig of water and squirted it through the gap between her front teeth. It landed in a neat little puddle on a stack of get-well cards. "Bull's-eye!" she said.

The next day a Pink Lady pushed a cart full of books into our room and parked it between our beds.

"Do we have another good reader in this room?" she

45

asked, smiling at me. "Pick out any book you like, dear. You can keep it until Tuesday."

I looked at the books on her cart. They were mostly picture books and the skinny kinds of books that Yoyo reads.

"These are all kids' books," I said.

"This *is* a children's hospital, dear," she said. "But I can get a special book for you from the library. Why, just last week I borrowed a book about the history of newspapers for your roommate."

Angie smiled.

"And the week before . . . ."

"Don't tell me," I said. "I bet she wanted a book about Abraham Lincoln."

"Why, that's right!" She turned to Angie. "What special subject are you interested in this week?"

"Sex," Angie said.

The Pink Lady didn't bat an eye. "I think I have something right here for you." She pulled out a skinny blue book with a picture of a baby, a chick, and a kitten on the cover.

Angie thumbed through the book. There were a lot of pictures, and the letters were about six inches high.

"This isn't exactly what I had in mind," she said. "I'd like something more *mature*."

"Perhaps *Everything You Always Wanted to Know About Sex But Were Afraid To Ask*," I suggested, remembering a title in Mother's headboard.

"That would be perfect," Angie said.

The Pink Lady blinked her eyes, then searched for that speck on the ceiling.

"I'm not sure I can get that book for you, Angie," she said.

"Just try." Angie smiled at her, and the Pink Lady backed out of the room. Then she turned to me. "You're catching on."

I touched my nose with my tongue

9

My first week at Franklin has been a lot like the week I spent at Girl Scout camp two years ago. Oh, I don't have poison ivy, and my bunkmate hasn't thrown up in the middle of the night. But it's been pretty bad all the same.

When Dr. Boggs brought his troop in for Friday morning inspection, I asked him when I could go home.

"At this point, it's difficult to say," he said.

"If it's all the same to you, I'd like to go home tomorrow."

"Tomorrow?"

"My parents are coming then, and I'd like to save them an extra trip."

Dr. Boggs smiled. "How considerate. I'm afraid, though, that we haven't made enough progress in your treatment to even consider discharging you."

So much for Dr. Boggs. But I still had my parents. Angie told me she once had a roommate whose parents pulled her out of the hospital despite the doctors' objections.

"What made them do it?" I asked.

"They said the hospital was doing her more harm than good," she said. "They had quite a battle with the doctors, though."

I wondered whether my parents were up to that sort of heroics.

Our menus came that afternoon so we could check off whether we wanted apple betty or fruit compote for dessert Saturday night. I noticed the main dish was going to be roast beef. We used to eat better on visiting day at camp, too.

Angie's mother arrived first on Saturday, only I didn't know she was her mother at first. She looked more like a grandmother, with gray streaks in her hair and a wrinkly face.

Mrs. Salvadore smiled and said hello when Angie introduced me. Then she turned and talked with Angie so quietly that I couldn't hear half of what they said. I didn't care, though. My own family would come soon.

Mother and Daddy would probably run into the room and hug me. Yoyo would stand back a little because she'd be overcome by the fact that her big sister was in a hospital. Besides, Yoyo's not much for hugging.

After our emotional greeting, I'd begin dropping hints about the damage that five days in the hospital had done to my body and soul. Mother and Daddy would hug me again and begin packing my suitcase.

It didn't turn out that way.

To begin with, Mother and Daddy didn't run into the room. Mother walked in by herself. She did hug me, though.

"Where's everyone else?" I asked.

"Daddy is downstairs with Yolanda," she said. "Poor Yolanda. The hospital won't let her come see you."

"Why not? Her personality?" I just couldn't resist saying that.

Mother ignored my comment. "I can understand why visitors have to be thirteen years old in a hospital for adults. But here, in a children's hospital, I don't see what harm a mature nine-year-old girl could do."

If Mother could ignore my comment about Yoyo's personality, I could ignore hers about Yoyo's maturity.

"Enough about Yolanda," Mother said. "How have you been?"

I remembered my plan. "Not so good."

Mother examined me. "You do look different," she said. "But I thought it was the glasses."

I shook my head. "I seem to be getting worse."

"How do you mean?"

"For one thing, I can't walk at all anymore."

"What?"

I nodded. "It's true. I have to stay in the wheelchair all day. Either that or in bed."

Mother glanced at the walker beside my bed.

I thought fast. "That belongs to Angie."

Mother looked at the other walker by Angie's bed. I pretended not to notice.

"I'm sure Dr. Boggs knows what he's doing," Mother said.

"I hope so. Of course, if he doesn't, we can always file a malpractice suit later."

Mother spotted two yarn dolls on my night table. "Did you make those? Dr. Cosley said you'd have occupational therapy here."

I took a deep breath. "No, Angie made those."

"Angie seems to have been pretty busy."

"Yes, it's hard on her, with the bedpans and all." As long as I'd gone this far, I might as well finish.

"Bedpans?"

"I don't like to bother the nurses all the time, and I'm not allowed out of bed."

"What about the wheelchair? Doesn't it fit through the bathroom door?"

This was getting hard. "I'm only allowed in the wheelchair for long trips."

"Long trips?"

"You know, like when I get out of here. They'll take me out in a wheelchair. Either that or a stretcher."

"Oh."

She said she had to leave so Daddy could come up.

After she left, I thought about the rough spots in my story. It was a good thing Mother had come up first so I could practice my story on her. Daddy's pretty sharp, and he might have caught on.

When Daddy came in, he hugged me and said, "I hear you don't want to stay here."

"I never said that."

"You gave that impression."

"I didn't think Mother . . . ."

"Caught on? Listen, honey, she works with four-year-olds every day. Don't you think she recognizes a whopper when she hears one?"

Later in the afternoon Daddy took Yoyo into the hospital courtyard while I watched from Angie's window. They counted the hospital floors, then the windows. When Yoyo spotted me, she started jumping up and down and waving both arms.

I wonder if she knows how lucky she is to have legs that bounce and bend like that.

Somebody should tell her.

10

I'm getting fat. Angie was the first one to notice it.

"You must really like the food here," she said.

"It's okay."

"You seem to be putting on a little weight."

I opened my secret hiding place and looked in the mirror. My face was puffy.

"Don't worry about it," Angie said. "You look cute."

But when Wendy came in, she looked at me hard.

"Were you wearing glasses the first time I met you?" she asked.

"No."

"Take them off."

I did, and she shook her head. "You still look different," she said. "I didn't think your face was so . . . ."

"Full?" Angie provided the word.

"That's a nice way of putting it," Wendy said. "You really should go on a diet, Jenna. You can't let yourself go to pot here."

I didn't eat the grilled cheese sandwich at lunch, and I only had a salad and a glass of milk for supper. I filled up on water.

All the water did was make me go to the bathroom. I was still hungry, and my stomach growled for food.

By the time Mrs. Ruth came in for back rubs, the growls had turned to roars. At first we both pretended not to notice.

"I guess you're sorry you didn't eat today," Mrs. Ruth finally said.

"How did you know I didn't eat?"

"I looked at your chart."

"You people put everything on charts."

"We try to," she said. "Would you like a snack now?"

"Don't tempt me. I'm trying to lose weight."

"What?"

"Haven't you noticed how fat I'm getting? Look at me." I held up my hands. "Even my fingers look puffy."

She smiled. "You're not getting fat, Jenna."

"Oh, no? Even Angie noticed it."

"You're beginning to look a little puffy because of the medicine you've been taking. Cortisone always makes people look swollen."

"Well, then I'm not going to take any more of it."

"You need cortisone to treat your arthritis."

"Forget it," I said. "I'm not going to take any more."

"Would you rather look a little puffy or spend the rest of your life in a wheelchair?"

What a choice.

"If I were you," Angie said. "I'd take puffy."

I looked at her. "Of course you would," I said. "You're so skinny that a little puffiness wouldn't hurt."

Angie licked her finger and gave me a point in the air. "Just call me Bones," she said, "and I'll call you Puff."

Maybe it's the cortisone or maybe it's Ross's exercises, but something is beginning to make my legs work better. Sometimes I can bend my knees a little without feeling that hot knife slice through them. Not all the time, but sometimes.

52

I told Ross and he said I'd probably be ready for crutches pretty soon.

"Good," I said. "Then I won't have to mess with that stupid walker anymore."

"If it weren't for that 'stupid walker,' you'd be in a lot worse shape today," he said.

"Huh?"

"How many times has it kept you from falling? Three or four times? Ten times? Twenty?"

"I don't know. Why?"

"Just one good fall could destroy all the progress you've made so far."

I gripped the walker tighter. I want to get rid of that hot knife forever.

When I got back from therapy, Angie and Wendy were examining a box on the chair by the TV. As soon as I saw the Girl Scout stickers plastered all over it, I knew what the package must be.

"It's probably a Sunshine Box," Wendy said.

I nodded. My old troop once made a Sunshine Box for a kid who fell out of a tree and broke his leg. He never sent us a thank-you note, and we never made another Sunshine Box. Yoyo's troop must have held a special summer meeting to make this, so I'll be sure to send them a nice thank-you letter.

"Aren't you going to open it?" Wendy asked.

I tore off the brown wrapping paper and found a white box decorated with messages written in green ink. Most of them said "Good Luck," "Get Well Soon," or "We Miss You."

I didn't recognize the names of a couple of kids who missed me.

But I sure recognized Jennifer Steeple's name. She was

supposed to spend the night with Yoyo a few weeks ago, but she started crying for her mommy around ten o'clock, so Daddy had to drive her home. What a baby.

Jennifer had written a poem on the bottom of the box:

> Roses are red.
> Violets are blue.
> You may walk funny,
> But we still like you.

I didn't read that one aloud. Wendy would have enjoyed it too much.

Inside the box were several smaller packages wrapped in green tissue paper. I tossed aside the hot-pink handkerchief and the Wonder Woman comic book. Some nine-year-olds have terrible taste.

There was a bag of potato chips, and we ate about half of them.

"Let's save the rest for later," Angie said. "We don't get stuff like this very often, and we shouldn't eat it all at once."

"Okay, but don't eat any when I'm not here," Wendy said. I wondered whose Sunshine Box she thought this was.

Another package contained a pair of terrycloth slippers made out of two washcloths. I knew the elastic wouldn't stretch over my swollen feet, so I didn't even try.

"This Sunshine Box is okay," Wendy said, "but it's not half as stupid as mine was." She made stupid Sunshine Boxes sound like a wonderful thing.

The last package contained paper, sticks, and string for a kite.

"A kite!" Wendy hooted. "What will you ever do with a kite?"

"Tie it on your wheelchair and race down the hall," Angie suggested. "Anderson would like that.

"Your Sunshine Box is turning out o be pretty stupid after all," Wendy said approvingly. We all giggled.

That's when we heard it. The loud wail from across the hall.

11

"Get out of here!" Bill yelled. "Get out of here!"

Some grown-up voices tried to reason with him.

"Get out of here! All of you! Now!"

Sam shuffled into our room while the grownups gathered in the hall.

"What happened, Sam?" Angie asked.

"Bill just found out he has to have his leg amputated."

"Oh, my God."

"Why?"

"I'm not sure. Something about a mal-lig-auntsy."

"Malignancy." Wendy nodded. "That'll get 'em every time."

"Who's with Bill now?" Angie asked.

"Nobody. He chased us all out."

Angie reached for her walker.

"Where are you going?" I asked.

"To see Bill."

"He doesn't want to see you, or anybody else," Sam warned.

"I know."

We heard her knock on Bill's closed door. He didn't answer.

"Bill?"

"Go away!"

"Bill, it's me, Angie. And I won't go away."

"He doesn't want to talk to anyone right now," a grown-up voice said.

"He'll talk to me," Angie said.

"Oh, let her try," another grownup said.

Angie went inside and closed the door behind her. We waited for Bill to throw her out, but he let her stay.

"What a busybody," Wendy said.

"Maybe she'll make him feel better," I said.

Wendy shook her head. "Nothing will make him feel better."

When Bill came out of surgery, we knew as much about his recovery as his parents did. They had to rely on doctors for information. We had Sam.

I wheeled down to the nurses' station after lunch and asked how Bill was doing. Anderson told me not to worry about things that didn't concern me.

I reported what she said to Angie and Wendy.

"You mean you *asked* how Bill was doing?" Wendy said.

"Jenna hasn't been here very long," Angie explained. "We'd better get Sam."

They both yelled for Sam, and the kid popped out of his room and into ours.

"We think it's time to find out about Bill," Angie said. Sam nodded and left the room.

About five minutes later he returned. "Bill's out of surgery. He'll be in recovery for another hour or so."

"How did you find out?" I asked. "Anderson wouldn't tell me a thing."

"Jenna *asked* Anderson how Bill was doing," Wendy said.

"You're kidding." Sam shook his head. "You never ask

Anderson anything. You just hang around the nurses' station and listen. If you keep your mouth shut, pretty soon they forget you're there and they spill everything."

For a little kid, Sam is pretty smart.

He hung around the nurses' station until Bill's stretcher was wheeled into their room. Then Sam became very tired and decided to take a nap, with his ears open.

He came back to our room just before the dinner trays arrived.

"Bill threw up once, but otherwise he's okay," Sam said. "He won't talk to his dad, though. He just stares at the ceiling and won't say anything. It's spooky."

"He'll get over it," Angie said.

"Maybe not," said Wendy, staring at her own frozen legs. "He's just another loser."

"He's not a loser!" Sam shouted. "Have you ever seen the way he handles a basketball?"

Wendy laughed. "And how many one-legged basketball players do you know?"

Sam looked like he might cry, but Angie said, "Some colleges have wheelchair basketball teams."

"They'll probably give him an artificial leg, so he won't even qualify for that. What a loser." Wendy looked around the room. "This whole place is full of losers."

"What do you mean?" I asked.

"I mean," she said, in the same tone of voice I use when I'm explaining something obvious to Yoyo, "that if you're sick enough to be here, you might as well forget about basketball and everything else."

"Oh, Wendy . . .," Angie began, but Wendy waved her off, and she went on talking to me.

"Angie will *always* be passing out, Sam will *always* . . . what's wrong with you anyway, Sam?"

58

"I'm not exactly sure," he said. "I think there's something wrong with my brain."

Nobody fell for the cheap joke.

"Well, Sam will *always* have a sick head, and you," she said, looking at me, "will *always* be crippled."

There was that word again.

"I'm going down to the sunroom," I said.

When I came back, Angie was alone.

"You shouldn't let Wendy bother you," she said.

"She doesn't."

"She only says those things because she's feeling sorry for herself."

"I thought you said she doesn't want people to feel sorry for her."

"She doesn't. There's a difference between feeling sorry for yourself and having other people feel sorry for you. *You* should understand that."

"What's that supposed to mean? I don't feel sorry for myself."

"Oh, no? Then why did you leave when Wendy called you a cripple? Why do you always hide your legs behind that stupid afghan? Why do you . . . ."

"Okay, okay. But don't you ever feel sorry for yourself?"

Angie hesitated. "I used to. But not anymore. I don't have time for that anymore."

That didn't make sense. From what I've seen, Angie never has to go to physical therapy or the Shoe Box or anything. She just stays in our room all day, takes some medicine now and then, and keeps the Vampire stocked with blood.

Angie looked at the Sunshine Box, still sitting on the chair by my bed.

"I think you should put together that kite," she said.

59

"What for?"

"So you could put it on the wall . . ."

"Anderson would like that."

". . . and see it all the time. Maybe you'd stop worrying about what's wrong with you and start making plans to fly it."

"I can't fly a kite. You have to *run* to get a kite up in the air."

"Okay, maybe you can't fly it today. So what? You can make it today and look forward to flying it someday."

"Oh, boy."

"Don't knock it, Jenna. Everybody needs something to look forward to."

Wendy is right about one thing. Angie sure is a busy-body.

12

I get more mail than Angie and Wendy combined. Wendy says it's because I haven't been here long.

"Everybody sends letters when you first go to the hospital," she said. "Then they forget about you and don't write anymore."

"Oh, some people don't forget," Angie said. "I get a card twice a week from a lady I don't even know. I think she got my name and address out of the church bulletin."

So far, my mail has been more personal, maybe because we don't belong to a church.

Monday

Dear Jenna,

We all miss you terribly. Yolanda is especially lonely without her big sister. She was *so* disappointed when she couldn't come up to see you over the weekend. Jennifer Steeple's mother has invited her to spend next weekend with them, but I think we'll let her come to the hospital again. I hope to arrange special permission for her to visit you in your room. Wouldn't that be nice?

How is Angie? She looked so thin, the poor thing.

Do you know what's wrong with her? Her parents must be very worried.

Take care of yourself. And try to develop a more positive attitude toward the hospital staff. I'm sure Mrs. Anderson doesn't really take a swig of turpentine before she comes on duty.

Love,
Mother

P.S. I'm glad to see that you're wearing your glasses. You really do look quite nice in them.

Monday

Dear Jenna,

How are you? I'm fine. That was me, waving.

I'm sorry I couldn't come up to your room. The lobby was the pits. Mother wants me to go to the hospital again next weekend, but I want to stay with Jennifer Steeple. She says she won't cry at night if we're at her house. When we call Wednesday night, would you please tell Mother that you don't want me to come?

Did you get the Sunshine Box? I put the kite in. When you get home, I'll fly it for you.

Sincerely,
Yolanda Marie Matthews

P.S. Don't tell Mother I told you that we're going to call Wednesday. It's supposed to be a surprise.

Tuesday

Dear Jenna,

Please excuse the note paper. My grandmother gave it to me, and I've got to use it up.

Joe K. was at the pool yesterday, and he asked how you were. When we told him, he said, "That's too bad." Sunny is right. I think he likes you.

Guess what! I've decided to become a doctor! I thought about it for a long time, and your illness made me decide to go ahead and do it. I'll have to finish college first.

Love until Niagara Falls,

Celia

P.S. Grandma wants to know if the hospital has given you a copper bracelet. She wears one all the time, and she says it's done wonders for her arthritis.

Tuesday

Jenna—

Here's a little note, just to prove that city editors do so know how to write. Do what the doctors tell you so you can come home soon.

Love,

Daddy

Tuesday

Dear Jenna,

How are you? I'm OK except my you-know-what is late. It was supposed to start two days ago. I just know it will start at the pool. How will I get to the bathroom? Mom says it's normal to be irregular at first, but she doesn't understand at all.

We all miss you! Celia and I have both noticed how Joe K. has been pinning (sp?) away ever since he heard about your illness. It's so romantic!!!

Love until Niagara Falls,

Sunny

Wednesday

Dear Jenna,

How are you? I'm fine. Thanks a lot for fixing things with Mother about this weekend.

Jennifer Steeple and I went to the pool today. I couldn't find my bathing suit, so I borrowed yours. It fit pretty good. I snagged it on the counter at the snack stand, and it made a teeny tiny hole. Don't worry. It doesn't show at all if you don't raise your arms.

Sincerely,
Yolanda Marie Matthews

P.S. It's okay for you to call me Yoyo. Coach Thompson wants me to use that name in competition. He thinks I've got a good chance at a state medal in my age group this year.

Wednesday
Dear Jenna,

I'm surprised at you! Yolanda is dying to see you, and you say you don't care whether she comes or not. I just wish she hadn't been listening on the upstairs extension. She was very brave about it, but I know she was deeply hurt. You should write her and apologize.

I'm sorry to hear about the boy across the hall. He must be very depressed about his leg. I hope the hospital staff can help him adjust.

We'll see you Saturday.

Love,
Mother

Wednesday
Dear Jenna,

Will you please tell Sunny and Celia you got a letter from me? They've been bugging me to write you, and I want them to know I finally did it.

Joe Korth

P.S. Get well soon.

13

Mother and Daddy came early Saturday, before Angie's mother arrived.

"Did you get my letter?" Mother asked.

"You mean the one where you bawled me out about Yoyo?"

Mother nodded. "After I mailed it, Yolanda explained everything. I felt terrible."

"That's okay." As long as she was sorry, I could be generous.

"I felt so bad that I decided to arrange a special surprise for you."

"A surprise?"

"You wait right here." She and Daddy left.

I wondered what kind of surprise they could arrange. It was probably Yoyo. I bet they dragged her, kicking and screaming, all the way from Jennifer Steeple's house.

Then I heard giggling in the hall. It wasn't Yoyo. I tucked the afghan around my legs.

"SURPRISE!" Sunny and Celia bounced into the room.

I blinked. I hadn't seen regular kids in regular clothes since I'd gotten here.

"See?" Sunny said to Celia. "I told you she'd be surprised."

I could hardly talk. "How . . . how did you get here?"

"Your parents brought us," Celia said. Then she giggled. "And we told the nurse we were thirteen."

Sunny thrust out her chest. "Don't I look it?"

They laughed. They were very loud and they moved very fast. Much faster than Angie.

"Do you notice anything different, Jen?" Sunny held out her arms and spun around.

A lot was different, but I couldn't explain it.

"My tan, dummy!" she said. "I tried sunscreen, of all things. No more cocoa butter for me! See, I'm even darker than you." Sunny held her arm next to mine. "You look like a ghost."

"Sunny." Celia giggled.

But Sunny was right. My fantastic tan was gone. And I hadn't even noticed.

"Jenna knows I'm kidding. Don't you, Jen?" Sunny cocked her head and looked at me. "Do you wear glasses all the time now?"

I'd forgotten about them. "Do you like them?"

"They make you look brainy."

"Oh, no."

"I think they're cute," Celia said. "And you don't have to squint anymore."

I never knew I squinted.

Sunny sat down in the wheelchair by my bed. She patted the wheels at her side. "You don't use this thing, do you, Jen?"

"Not very often," I said. "Everyone uses one when they go to x-rays or therapy or something. It's a hospital rule."

"And what's this thing?" Celia asked, running a finger across the top bar of my walker.

"It's a walker."

"A what?" Sunny got up and took hold of the metal contraption.

"A walker."

"How do you use it?"

I told her, and she scooted it around the room.

"I don't see how it can help people walk," she said. "It just gets in the way."

"It takes practice," I said.

"They sure give you a lot of stuff to help you get around," Sunny said. "If you're not careful, you'll forget how to walk by yourself."

"Sunny." This time Celia wasn't giggling. She turned to me. "Do your legs still hurt?"

I shrugged. How could I describe the way my knees feel? "I'm taking some medicine that seems to help," I said.

"Yes, your mother warned us about the medicine," Sunny said.

"*Warned* you?"

"She wanted us to know it makes you look a little . . . different."

I looked at my puffy wrists.

"But if she hadn't told us, I never would have noticed," Celia said. "Would you, Sunny?"

"Hardly at all." Sunny smiled as if she were selling a toothpaste guaranteed to rot your teeth.

"Will you be able to go to school?" Celia asked.

"I think so."

"Will you have to use that thing?" She nodded toward the walker.

"I'm learning to use crutches."

"You poor thing," she murmured.

"How will you climb the bleachers at football games?" Sunny asked.

"Football games?"

"Don't tell me you've forgotten about the high school football games." Sunny looked as though I'd forgotten Christmas. "Junior high kids *always* sit at the top of the bleachers. It's tradition."

"Oh, that's right," I said. "Well, I guess I'll just have to sit near the bottom."

"With the old folks?"

"That's okay," Celia said. "We can take turns sitting with you."

"But all the boys sit at the top," Sunny said.

"We'll take turns," Celia said firmly. "Won't we, Sunny?"

"I guess so."

"We'll take turns at everything," Celia said. "We'll even take turns sitting with you at the dances after the games."

Sunny looked like her stomach hurt.

"We'll help you carry your books at school, too," Celia said. "We'll have to get out of classes early. You know what they say about the halls between classes. They're absolutely mobbed with kids rushing around, yelling and everything."

Kids rushing through halls, climbing bleachers, dancing. It all used to sound so exciting. Now it sounded . . . dangerous. What if somebody knocked me over? Hurt my knees?

Maybe I shouldn't go back to school, I thought. Maybe I should get a tutor, like Wendy had last year.

"You don't have to worry about a thing," Celia said. "We'll take care of you, won't we, Sunny?"

"Uh-huh."

I looked over at Angie. Her mother still hadn't come, and

she was concentrating on something in the courtyard beneath her window.

"I'm sorry," I said. "I forgot to introduce my roommate, Angie Salvadore. Angie, I've told you about Sunny and Celia."

"I didn't know they were so helpful," Angie said.

Celia smiled. "It's nothing."

"It'll be worse than nothing if you go through with it," Angie said.

Celia's mouth fell open. So did mine.

After they left, I turned on Angie. "What did you mean by telling Celia her help was worse than nothing?"

"Couldn't you see how sorry she felt for you?" Angie asked.

"She's only trying to help."

Angie shrugged. "It's up to you, whether you want to be her friend or her pet project."

14

Bill was shooting baskets again.

At first we were glad to hear the thud of his ball into the wastebasket.

"He's snapping out of it," Angie said.

"He'll be up and around in no time," I agreed.

But one afternoon he went on for three hours straight.

Thud into the basket. Rattle of Sam scooping it out. Whack back to Bill. Thud, rattle, whack. Thud. . . .

"It's driving me crazy," Wendy said.

"It's probably quieter in your room," I hinted. For somebody whose parents—or lawsuits—were spending so much money on a private room, Wendy sure didn't use it much.

Sam was the one who finally made Bill quit.

"Get yourself another ball boy!" he yelled as he stomped out of their room and into ours.

The moment I saw Sam, I forgot about Bill. The kid was wearing a red stocking cap with a picture of Charlie Brown on the front.

"What's with the cap?" Wendy asked. "Did they take your bandages off?"

He nodded. "Want to see?"

We all shook our heads, but he pulled off the cap anyway.

He looked like a little old man with a wrinkled scalp. Then he turned around. A bright red scar ran down the back of his head.

I shut my eyes.

"Can you see my stitches?" he asked. "I had twenty-seven of them."

Wendy breathed one word: "Gross."

"Put your hat on," Angie said weakly.

"Will your hair grow back?" Wendy asked.

"Yeah."

"Good. That will cover the scar. Until then, though, you'll need a toupe."

"What's a toupe?"

"A wig," Wendy said. "You can't walk around all summer with a stocking cap on."

"Oh, I don't know," Angie said. "I think he looks kind of cute."

"Cute." Wendy considered it. "No, I think it's more like dumb."

Angie changed the subject. "How's Bill?"

Sam rolled his eyes. "He gives me the spooks. He won't talk or nothin'. He just keeps throwing that basketball."

Angie nodded. "He's had it rough."

We were all quiet for a moment, thinking about Bill.

Sam shook his head. "You guys are no fun, either." He headed toward the door but stopped. "Unless you got something to eat?"

"Don't look at me," I said. "We finished the potato chips a long time ago."

"Too bad," Sam said. "I'm tired of all that nutritious slop the hospital gives us. Some junk food sure would taste good right now."

"I'd like something salty—pretzels or corn chips," I said.

"Personally, I'd prefer sour cream and onion potato chips," Wendy said.

Sam held his stomach and moaned.

"I know where there's some good junk food," Angie said. "There's a snack machine in the lounge on the other side of those glass doors."

"Too bad the doors are locked," I said.

"What makes you think they're locked?" Sam asked.

"I tried opening them once."

"Did you try the latch up at the top of the door?" he asked.

"I didn't know there was a latch up there."

"You're not supposed to know," he said. "They don't want kids running in and out all the time. But I bet I could reach the latch if I stood on somebody's wheelchair."

I offered mine.

We all rummaged through our secret hiding places and came up with $3.17. Sam pocketed the money in his bathrobe, and we all went out into the hall.

There were a lot of kids walking and wheeling down the corridor, but no nurses. Wendy kept watch while Angie and I held the wheelchair steady for Sam to climb up and release the latch. When it clicked open, he jumped down, opened the door, and escaped.

The rest of us went back to our room and waited about ten minutes.

"It shouldn't take him this long," Angie said. "He must be lost."

"Don't worry about Sam," I said. "He's a smart kid."

But fifteen minutes later even I wasn't sure of Sam's smarts. Angie reached for her walker.

"I'd better go find him," she said.

Wendy and I waited another ten minutes. Finally Sam came in by himself.

"We're in big trouble, you guys," he said. "Angie fell over in the hall, and I couldn't get her to move."

"So you just left her there?" I practically screamed at him.

"What else could I do? I couldn't carry her." He opened his bathrobe, and five or six little bags of potato chips fell out. "At least I got the stuff."

I reached for the call button, but Wendy grabbed my wrist.

"Don't be stupid," she said. "Somebody will find her and bring her back."

"Or maybe she'll wake up and come back by herself," Sam said.

I pressed the button. No one answered.

A crowd of white-uniformed people brought Angie in on a stretcher. Anderson was with them, shooting angry looks at Wendy and me.

"It's not our fault," Wendy said. "It was Angie's idea to go."

"We'll talk about this later," Anderson snapped. She yanked the curtain shut between our beds so we couldn't see Angie any more. An orderly wheeled in a gray wired box, and a strange doctor ran into the room.

"What's going on?" I whispered to Wendy.

"She's just passed out again. There's nothing to worry about."

"But she's never been out this long. Why doesn't she wake up?"

"I don't know. Maybe she's just faking it so Anderson won't get mad at her."

If that was Angie's strategy, it worked. People kept fussing over her, even after she woke up. A nurse I'd never seen before stayed in our room all night and kept the curtain drawn between our beds. I wanted to open it, to make sure Angie was okay, but I didn't. The nurse didn't seem to know I was there, and I thought she might make me leave if I started doing things in the middle of the night.

I couldn't sleep, though. For one thing, that nurse kept talking. She'd wake up Angie and ask her dumb questions like what was her name and what grade was she in. Even I knew Angie was sick and needed to get some rest, but the woman just wouldn't leave her alone. You'd think a registered nurse would know better.

In the morning the nurse said Angie was feeling better, and she thought she'd like some company. I looked toward the door, but no one was coming. The nurse opened the curtain between our beds, and I saw that I was the company.

"Hi, Angie," I said.

"Hi."

She looked awful. Her lips were practically purple, and a tube was stuck in her nose. Her arm had a couple of needles in it that were hooked up to some bottles.

"Is Sam okay?" she asked.

"Uh-huh."

"Did he get anything?"

"Potato chips, but Wendy says they're stale."

Angie smiled. "That's Wendy."

I smiled back.

"I feel like a zombie," she said.

"You're just a little tired," the nurse said. "You'll feel better after you've had a nap. Then I'll fix your hair so you'll be pretty for your mother."

"But Mama's not coming until Saturday."

"Your doctor called her last night, and she decided to come see you today."

"Uh-oh."

"You poor kid," I said. "You must be awfully sick."

"That's enough nonsense, girls," said the nurse, closing the curtain between us. "Angela needs her rest."

"Can you wait just a minute?" A voice came from the door. I didn't recognize it until Bill wheeled himself in. I hadn't seen him since the day of the race.

"Sam says you had a close call yesterday," he said.

"I guess so. My mother's coming today."

"That's too bad."

We all sat there without saying anything. I think Bill and I were waiting for Angie to spout some of her busybody philosophy, but she didn't.

Finally Bill said, "I just wanted you to know that I'm okay now. I'm going to get fitted for an artificial leg today."

My eyes fell to his lap, where one leg of his pajamas was tied in a knot. I looked back at Angie, with a tube stuck up her nose.

I don't think I'll use Wendy's afghan anymore.

15

I'm no doctor, but I'm not a dummy, either.

Angie hasn't been the same since she came back from the snack machine. Even after they took the tube out of her nose, she stayed in bed all the time, except to go to the bathroom.

Anderson told her to buzz for help whenever she had to go, but Angie said she didn't like having someone stand over her when she was sitting on the pot.

"I need my privacy," she said as she reached for her walker.

Her broomstick legs were pretty wobbly, though, and even with the walker, they couldn't hold her up. She fell, and I buzzed for help. Jim carried her back to bed and lectured her about making solo trips to the john.

Angie always said she'd call for help the next time, but she never did.

Finally Anderson herself came in, with bad news on her face.

"Your doctor says your scar tissue needs more time to heal, and she wants you to avoid unnecessary motion," she said.

I looked at Angie. I didn't see any scar tissue.

"So we're going to take away your bathroom privileges for a while," Anderson said "You can use a bedpan."

Angie's eyes got real big. "A bedpan?"

Anderson nodded.

"I won't do it," Angie said.

"It's just a temporary measure," Anderson said.

"I still won't do it."

A nurse's aide brought her a bedpan every couple of hours, but Angie refused to use it. After a day of this, I marveled at her bladder capacity.

"I'd be bursting by now," I said.

"I think I'm going to." She looked like she was in real pain, but she pushed herself up to sit on the edge of her bed.

"What are you doing?" I asked.

"Going to the bathroom," she said as her feet dropped to the floor.

"You'd better not," I warned, but it was too late. She fell in a heap on the floor. I pressed the call button and when Jim picked her up, I saw a puddle where she had fallen.

Since then, Angie's been using the bedpan. A nurse always pulls the curtain shut between us, but I can still hear the tinkle on metal.

I know I shouldn't, but sometimes I get mad at Angie for being so sick. When I come back from therapy every day, I want to tell her about the way I walked between two bars without stumbling. I want to tell her what Ross says about all the improvement I've made. I want to show her my new crutches.

But then I see her, so skinny and quiet in bed. Just switching TV channels, drifting off to sleep, asking for a bedpan. I almost feel guilty about getting better.

Not guilty enough to give up any of the progress I've made, though. I felt like a kid with a new bike when Ross handed me the crutches. I never knew anybody who used a wheelchair or walker before I came to Franklin, but I've seen lots of people with crutches in the outside world. Even Daddy used a crutch for a few days after he sprained his ankle in a basketball game during his lunch hour.

I found out pretty fast that crutches aren't as easy to use as they look. They rubbed against my arms until I got blisters, and my hands were sore from clutching the handles. Ross says I have to learn to relax with them, but I keep remembering what he said about falling, so I hold on tight.

Ross says I might use a cane this fall. I want to get a shiny black metal one, with a rhinestone-studded handle, the kind you'd expect a glamorous movie star to use if she sprained her ankle playing tennis.

I came back from therapy one morning and found Angie with her hair combed and the head of her bed raised so she was almost sitting up.

"You look a lot better today," I said.

"Thanks. So do you."

I guess she hadn't looked at me in a long time. So I brought her up to date. I told her about the crutches and the movie-star cane.

"I think you should get a white-tipped cane, like the ones blind people use," Angie said.

"Why?"

"So people will look at your eyes and forget about your legs."

It was nice to have Angie feeling better and back in the busybody business.

But it didn't last. The next morning she was quiet and

kept drifting off to sleep again.

Sometimes I think Angie's never going to leave that bed by the window. Everybody else seems to think that way, too. Her mother stopped working at the shoe store and rented a room across the street from the hospital.

Mrs. Salvadore comes every morning around ten o'clock and stays until after supper. She doesn't leave for lunch or anything. Whenever Angie closes her eyes, Mrs. Salvadore whips out some black rosary beads and makes the sign of the cross. She doesn't pray aloud, but I can see her lips move. Sometimes she prays on those beads six or seven times a day.

She's probably praying for Angie to get well. Or maybe she's just praying that Angie will eat something.

It's not that Angie doesn't try to eat. When our food trays arrive, Angie always presses the button to raise the head of her bed. Then she unwraps the silverware and starts jabbing at her food. Her hands are so shaky, though, that the food hardly ever makes it to her mouth. It falls on the sheets, the floor, and Angie's nightgown.

The nurse's aides always offer to feed Angie. Sometimes they cut up her meat and put a piece on her fork. But when they hold the fork to her mouth, Angie just sits there with tight lips and shakes her head at them.

Finally they give up and leave. Then Mrs. Salvadore tries. But Angie keeps her mouth shut.

"Oh, Angie," her mother says, so softly that I can hardly hear her. "Why won't you let us help you?"

Then Mrs. Salvadore sits back, and Angie starts jabbing and spilling.

"Why won't you let your mother feed you?" I asked one night after Mrs. Salvadore left. "You'd get a lot more food that way, and you wouldn't be so skinny."

"I like to do things myself," she said.

"But you make such a mess."

"If it bothers you, close the curtain."

Angie is getting to be very touchy. She even complains about things she should be grateful for.

"Why's everybody being so nice to me all of a sudden?" she asked after a nurse's aide cheerfully cleaned up an oatmeal mess one morning.

"You're just imagining things," I told her. "Everyone treats you the same as always."

"Oh, yeah? Watch this."

She pressed the call button and asked Anderson to come.

"What's wrong?" the voice in the speaker asked.

"I don't know," Angie said. "I just feel awful. Could you come?"

Anderson ran to our room, her basketball breasts pumping for air.

"What's wrong?" she asked, taking hold of Angie's wrist.

"I don't know. Could I have a drink of water?"

Anderson poured water from the pitcher on Angie's night table and held it to her lips.

"Jenna needs some water, too. Could you pour it for her?"

Anderson looked at me, and I smiled. I had no idea what Angie was up to.

"Jenna can pour her own water," Anderson said.

"Here, Jenna, you can have some of mine." Angie held out her cup and dropped it. The plastic cup cracked and water splashed across the floor.

"Oh, dear," Anderson said in an even voice. "I'll send someone in to clean this up."

She left, and Angie turned to me. "See what I mean? If anyone else had done that, Anderson would have hit the ceiling." She sighed. "I wish somebody would yell at me again."

16

Just before they left Sunday afternoon. Mother announced that she and Daddy would be back Wednesday morning. I figured things must be pretty bad if they were going to take a day off from work and drive a hundred miles to see me.

I was right. Things were bad. They wanted to talk with Dr. Boggs.

Their appointment with Dr. Boggs reminded me of the forty-seven minutes they spent with Dr. Cosley. I decided I'd better sit in on this conference, just to protect my own interests.

"I don't think that would be wise, dear," Mother said. "The doctor might not feel free to talk with you there."

"Why not? You'll be talking about me."

"You know how some grownups are," Daddy said. "They don't talk straight around kids."

I nodded.

"This way we'll be able to get all the facts, and we'll pass them on to you," he said.

"We'll tell you everything," Mother promised.

They were both smiling when they returned from the conference.

"Dr. Boggs says you're doing very well," Mother said. "He

wants us to go to therapy with you this afternoon so we can learn how to help you with your exercises. And you know what that means."

"I'll be going home soon!"

We all laughed and hugged each other.

In the excitement, Daddy said, "And you won't have to have an operation after all!"

The laughter and hugging stopped.

"What operation?"

Daddy looked uncertainly at Mother, and she frowned.

"You know," he said, "the operation we thought you might need."

"No, I didn't know. Why didn't you tell me?"

They exchanged glances, and Mother took the lead.

"Because we thought you might not have to have surgery, and if you didn't, what would be the point in worrying you about it? As it turned out, we were right. You didn't have to have an operation, and you didn't have to worry."

"But I have a right to worry about my own body! When are you guys going to stop treating me like a baby?"

They looked at each other again.

"You're right, Jenna," Daddy said. "We should have told you about the surgery. From now on, we'll tell you everything."

"Everything?"

"Everything," he promised.

"What else did the doctor say?"

"Not much."

"There you go again!"

"All right," Daddy said. "We talked about your future."

"My future?"

"The possibility of your knees getting worse."

"Worse? I thought they were getting better."

"They are, they are." He smiled, then looked away. "But they could get bad in the future."

"When?"

"I don't know."

"Would you like to go for a walk, dear?" Mother picked up my crutches.

"No! I want to know what's going to happen to me."

"We don't know," Daddy said. "Nobody knows. Some kids recover from arthritis and never have any more problems with it. Others keep getting worse."

"Then what's the point of working so hard at those exercises?"

"Those exercises, along with the medicine you take, help minimize the damage done by the arthritis," he said. "And that's all there is to tell. Honest."

"Now how about that walk?" Mother was still holding the crutches.

"I don't feel like it." I folded my arms and put on a pretty good pout.

"I wish you'd cheer up," Mother said. "The doctor says it's important for you to have an optimistic attitude."

"I'm optimistic, all right," I said sourly.

Mother glanced over at Angie. Her eyes were closed, and Mrs. Salvadore's head was bowed over her rosary beads.

"Maybe you ought to change rooms," Mother said.

"What's wrong with this one?"

"You need a cheerful setting." Mother looked over at Angie again. "And Angie is so sick."

"She's just got funny blood. I'm not going to catch anything."

"That's not what I meant."

"Well, I'm not moving, so you can forget about that!"

I don't know whether Angie heard Mother. If she did, she didn't say anything about it. But then, Angie doesn't say much of anything any more. Maybe it's because she's sick. Or maybe it's because her mother is around so much.

In the evening, after Mrs. Salvadore left, Bill walked into our room with his new leg and crutches. Sam stood at the door, but Bill motioned him in.

"The kid thinks you're mad at him," Bill told Angie.

"What for?"

"He thinks you wouldn't have gotten so sick if you hadn't gone to look for him that day."

"Is that what you think?" Angie asked Sam. He nodded.

"That's just silly," she said. "I've been sick for almost two years, and I don't think anyone can do anything to help me *or* hurt me."

"Honest?"

"Honest."

"Boy, I'm glad to hear that!" Sam started to leave. He waited, though, when he saw Bill was staying. Bill shooed him away.

"I'm leaving tomorrow," Bill said.

"We'll miss you," Angie said, and I nodded.

"I wanted to thank you for helping me."

"I didn't think I did."

"Well, you did." Bill stared hard at that speck on the ceiling. "I just wish I could do something for you now."

We all stared at that speck pretty hard. I'm surprised it didn't fall.

Bill had to leave when we heard the tinkle of the priest's bell. Angie kept her eyes shut a long time after Communion. Even after she opened them, she didn't say anything. She turned down Mrs. Ruth's offer of a back rub, and she was quiet while my sleeping equipment was adjusted.

After the lights were out, she said, "I wonder what happens to people after they die."

She spoke so softly that I wasn't sure whether she was talking to me, but I answered anyway. "I suppose they go to heaven . . . or maybe hell."

"Don't you believe in purgatory?" she asked.

"What's that?"

"It's a place where people with little sins go. They burn off their sins there so they'll be clean enough to enter heaven."

"It sounds terrible," I said. "I don't think I believe in it."

"What do you think heaven is like?" she asked.

"Oh, I don't know. I've always pictured a bunch of ladies standing around in long white dresses and singing hallelujah."

"That sounds almost as bad as purgatory," Angie said.

All this talk about heaven and purgatory was giving me the spooks. "What's really wrong with you?" I asked.

"I told you, I have funny blood."

"How funny? As funny as . . . leukemia?" One of the kids at Humpty Dumpty had had leukemia, and he'd died.

"Lots of kids get leukemia," Angie said. "I've got something much weirder than that." She paused. "Blood keeps leaking out of capillaries in my head."

"Out of what?"

"Capillaries. They're like tiny veins."

"Oh." I thought about it. "How do you stop them from leaking?"

"I put ace bandages on them."

"Be serious," I said. "Can't your doctor do something?"

"She can't find which capillaries are leaking."

86

This was getting complicated. "If she can't find them, how does she know they're leaking?"

"I have blood in my spinal fluid."

"Doesn't everyone?"

Angie laughed. "You sure don't know much about the human body, do you?"

I didn't say anything.

"I'm sorry," she said. "I didn't know much about capillaries and spinal fluid before I got sick, either."

"How did they find out you had blood in your spinal fluid?"

"A doctor stuck a needle in my back and drained some out."

"Yuck. That must have hurt."

"Yeah. Only it didn't hurt as much as . . . ." She stopped.

"As much as what?"

She was quiet for a moment. "As much as my head."

"Does your head hurt?"

"Sometimes."

"You're kidding."

"Why? What's wrong?"

It was hard to explain. I mean, I knew she was sick, and I knew she was weak. But I never knew she had any *pain*. I wondered if her head ever hurt as much as my knees.

"What's wrong?" she asked again.

"Oh, nothing. It's just funny that I could live with you so long and not know that your head hurt."

17

Anderson came into our room wearing a big smile. It made her face look even fatter.

"Good morning, girls," she said.

We didn't commit ourselves to any friendly greetings.

"Angie's doctor thinks it would be a good idea for her to have a room of her own." She aimed her smile at Angie. "Won't that be fun, dear?"

"No." Angie still has a nice way of putting things.

"And, Jenna, we're expecting a nice little girl today who wants to be your roommate."

"How little?"

"Just a little bit younger than you. Nine years old, I believe."

Just a little bit younger? That's the same age as Yoyo!

"Why does the doctor want me to move?" Angie asked.

Anderson sucked in her breath, the way some people do before they tell a whopper. "So you'll be closer to the nurses' station. It's difficult to come all the way down here every time we have to check your I.V."

That made sense, sort of. Since Angie wasn't eating much with the jab-and-spill method, they had hooked her up to some bottles again.

"Why can't Jenna come with me?"

Anderson sucked in her breath again. "The only room available is a single."

"I don't want to go without Jenna," Angie said.

"Jenna can visit you anytime."

"I want to stay by my window."

"There's a window in your new room."

"Are you sure this is her doctor's idea?" I asked, thinking of my parents.

"Of course it is." The sweetness left her voice, and Anderson sounded more like her old self. "Angela is going to move today, and that's all there is to it. Jim!"

Jim appeared at the door with an empty hospital cart.

"You can start moving Angela's things," Anderson told him, and she marched out.

Jim took a suitcase out of Angie's locker and packed her nightgowns and underwear. Then he piled her craft projects, books, and all the other junk she hadn't touched in a couple of weeks into the cart. Finally, he peeled off each get-well card from the wreath over her bed.

"Don't worry," he told her. "I'll help you decorate your new pad. By tonight it'll look as bad as this one."

He wheeled the cart out of the room.

"I suppose he'll take me on his next trip," Angie said. "Then they'll change the sheets on the bed, and it'll be like I was never here."

"Don't say that. I'll miss you."

"I hope you like your new roommate."

"She's only nine."

"Some nine-year-olds are nice."

"When you get those bottles and tubes out of your arm, maybe you can come back to this room."

"By that time you'll be gone."

"I hope so." As soon as I said it, I was sorry. I moved over

89

to her bed and thought about holding her hand to comfort her. But that seemed too corny, so I just stood there.

Jim brought in a stretcher and a nurse's aide.

"Gee, I hate to break up such a great act," he said.

"Then don't," Angie said.

"Sorry, kid. I've got my orders."

The aide straightened the tube from Angie's arm so the bottle could reach over to a hook at the head of the stretcher. Jim lifted Angie onto the stretcher. For a moment her arms lay bare, and I saw how purple they were from needles sticking her. The aide tucked a sheet around her, and Angie turned to me.

"You can move over to the window bed now," she said.

"Are you sure you want me to?"

"I'd rather have you there than some nine-year-old." She grinned.

I tried to grin back, but my lips kept jumping around. "I'll come visit you."

After they left, another aide came in and ripped the sheets off Angie's bed.

"Do you want to move over here?" she asked.

I hesitated. Then I thought of the nine-year-old.

"Sure." I moved all the stuff out of my secret hiding place and into Angie's.

After the aide finished, I was alone in the room until an orderly took me down to therapy. When I got back, Wendy and Sam were waiting for me.

"They really moved her," Wendy said.

"Uh-huh." I lifted myself up onto Angie's bed and stared out the window. I didn't feel like talking.

"It doesn't seem right for you to be in Angie's bed," Wendy said.

"Why not?" asked Sam. "I'm in Bill's old bed."

"That's different," she said. "Bill went home. Angie's still here, in a private room. And we know what that means."

"No, we don't," I said. "You're in a private room."

"That's different."

"No, it's not!"

The door opened, and Jim wheeled in a little girl with thick brown braids.

"Jenna, this is your new roommate, Mavis," he said.

Mavis smiled. Two front teeth were missing.

"You're not nine years old," I said.

"Of course not," she lisped. "I'm six."

Oh, my God.

"The nurse said you'd be nine."

Mavis smiled a teacher's pet kind of smile. "Mommy says I'm very mature for my age."

Somebody groaned. I think it was Wendy.

Standing behind Mavis, Jim frowned and mouthed the words "Be nice." Then he said aloud, "Okay, everybody, it's almost time for lunch. Wendy, Sam, back to your rooms. Don't bother changing clothes before lunch, Mavis. You can wait until your mom gets here."

"Her mommy, you mean," Wendy said, on her way out.

"Hey, Jim." I stopped him from following the others. "Can I go see Angie after lunch?"

"Do you think you could wait until tomorrow? She's pretty tired after moving and all."

"How could she be tired? She just stayed on the stretcher, didn't she?"

"Yeah, but I think she's asleep now." He stepped out of the way of a woman carrying in lunch trays. "I'll see you later."

I didn't mean to get friendly with the shrimp who'd taken Angie's place. But when I saw that the lunch tray was too high for Mavis, I told her how to crank down the table that

91

swung over the bed. Then I showed her how to play with the bed buttons, turn off the TV, and call the nurse. She nodded respectfully at my knowledge, and I began to think I might be able to tolerate her presence in Angie's room after all.

Then her mother came.

"Ooh, isn't this nice?" Mommy said. "Mavis is so lucky to be sharing a room with a big girl."

Mavis nodded.

"If Mavis needs anything during the night, she can just ask her big-girl roommate. Jenna will be just like the big sister Mavis has always wanted."

I thought about telling Mommy what big sisters think of little sisters who bug them during the night.

Mommy stayed all afternoon, past suppertime. Every hour on the hour she reached into a bulging yellow tote bag and pulled out a surprise for Mavis. That kid took in one Barbie Doll, two Barbie Doll outfits, one toy stethoscope, two ruffled nightgowns, and a coloring book with a jumbo set of crayons.

When the loudspeaker in the hall said it was time for visitors to leave, Mommy and Mavis clung to each other and cried.

"My poor baby!" Mommy sobbed. I tried to look away, but Mommy flung herself at my bed. "Jenna, promise me that you'll look after Mavis. She's so little. I tried to get a single room so I could stay with her at night, but there aren't any available. You'll take care of her, won't you?"

"Okay."

That made Mavis cry all the harder. Probably because she knew I didn't have a bulging yellow tote bag.

Mrs. Ruth finally had to break them apart and send Mommy home. As soon as she was gone, Mavis dried up and watched "Happy Days" on TV.

During a commercial I asked her why she was in the hospital.

"I need tests," she said.

"Tests for what? What's wrong with you?"

"I need tests," she repeated.

I can't remember whether Yoyo was that dumb when she was six.

Mavis was okay until Mrs. Ruth fixed my sandbag trap and turned off the lights. Then she started bawling again. I wanted to stuff a pillow down her throat.

Then I remembered my first night at Franklin.

"I hated my first night here, too," I said. She was crying so loud that she didn't hear me. I repeated myself. This time she must have heard me because she shut up.

"When I first came here, I didn't know what it would be like, and I didn't know about the friends I'd make."

Mavis made a funny noise. I think she was trying to swallow a sob.

18

My legs are getting better and better.

I can whip along pretty fast on crutches now, and I'm learning to use a cane for short distances. For super short distances, I don't need to use anything at all.

And I know just what super short distance I want to walk. I want to stroll into Angie's room and watch her eyes pop open.

I haven't seen Angie since she moved. Every time I ask Jim if I can go see her, he says she's either resting or with her doctor.

I got tired of his excuses and decided to find Angie on my own. I figured she'd be easy to find, in a single room near the nurses' station, like Anderson said.

I used my crutches to walk down to the nurses' station. Sure enough, there was a single room right across the hall. I propped my crutches against the wall and walked in.

A kid about Sam's age was in bed.

"Where's Angie?" I asked.

"Who?"

"Angie Salvadore. She's supposed to be in this room."

"Never heard of her."

The kid must have been new. I picked up my crutches and checked the other rooms round the nurses' station. I asked everyone who was old enough to talk, but nobody knew where Angie was.

My arms ached from leaning on the crutches. But I kept looking, in rooms farther and farther away from the nurses' station. Finally I couldn't walk anymore. I spotted an empty wheelchair and sat down.

After a while I got up and started the long walk back to my room. I kept thinking about Angie and wondering where Anderson put her. Maybe I'd never see her again. Maybe . . . .

"Ooof!" I almost fell over when a wheelchair spun out of a room and into my path.

"Oh, hi," Wendy said.

Oh, hi? Was that all she could say? She could have knocked me over and sent my knees back to the beginning of July. I glared at her.

But Wendy didn't notice. "You should be more careful," she said, almost kindly. "You could fall and hurt yourself."

I stopped glaring. She didn't notice that, either.

"Where have you been, anyway?" she asked. "Your doctor came by with his hordes of interns, but no one could find you."

"I went to see Angie."

"How is she?"

"I don't know. I never found her."

"What do you mean?"

"Anderson said she had to move to a single room near the nurses' station, right?"

Wendy nodded.

"I looked, and she's not there. She's not in any of the rooms near there. I think there must be something wrong."

Wendy nodded again and told me to follow her. She wheeled back to her room and motioned for me to sit down next to her.

"Do you think she died?" she whispered.

"Wendy!"

"She's been awfully sick."

"But somebody would have told us."

"What would somebody have told us?" Sam walked into the room.

Wendy and I looked at each other.

"We were talking about Angie," I said. "I can't find where Anderson put her."

"Did you check the room chart at the nurses' station?" Sam asked.

"What room chart?"

Sam shook his head. "And I thought you were getting some smarts." He left and came back in a few minutes with the news that Angie was in room 301.

"Where's that?" I asked.

" 'Way down at the other end of the hall."

"How's that any closer to the nurses' station than our old room?"

Sam shrugged. "It's not."

"Well, I'm going to see her." I stood up. "Does anyone want to come along?"

"Not me," Sam said. "My doctor is supposed to come by in a little while to tell me when I can go home."

"I'll go," Wendy said.

I started to position my crutches under my sore arms, but I looked at Wendy's wheelchair and remembered how Angie used to push me around.

"Let me push you," I said.

"I can push myself quite well, thank you," she replied.

"I know, but if I could lean on your wheelchair, I wouldn't have to use my crutches."

Wendy looked at the crutches for a moment. "All right, if you want to."

I pushed Wendy all the way to the other end of the hall. We stopped outside 301 and peeked in.

The lights were off, and the shades were drawn. In a patch of light coming from the hall, we could see a large white hospital bed with a cot next to it. Mrs. Salvadore was sitting, with her head bowed, in a chair at the foot of the bed. The figure in bed was still.

"Angie's asleep," Wendy whispered. "Let's go."

"Wait a minute," I said. "What's the cot for? I thought this was supposed to be a single."

"Angie's mother is probably staying at night."

"And why is it so dark in there?" I asked. "Why doesn't her mother turn on some lights."

"I told you, Angie's asleep."

"She shouldn't sleep so much," I said. "Her mother should open the windows and turn on some lights. Angie's never going to get well in a place like this."

Wendy looked at me strangely. "Angie's never going to get well, period."

"Don't say that. Don't even think it."

She half smiled. "Let's go back to your room."

We got there just as Mommy was giving Mavis a loom for making potholders. We all raved over the way Mavis's talented little fingers picked up cloth loops and hooked them over the rungs of the loom.

"What a spoiled brat," Wendy said, under her breath. "Every time I see that kid, she's got something new."

"What did you say, dear?" Mommy turned toward Wendy.

"Uh...."

I spoke up. "Wendy was admiring the number of presents you've given Mavis since she's been here."

Mommy beamed. "I just want my little girl to be happy. You know the old saying: Busy hands are happy hands."

Mavis held up her loom for us to see. "Pretty?"

Mommy fell all over herself admiring Mavis's work. But I didn't listen. I was thinking about what she'd just said.

Busy hands are happy hands.

That's why Angie keeps getting sicker. Ever since she came back from the snack machine, she's been lying in bed, doing nothing. And that dark little room at the end of the hall just makes it worse.

"I've got it!" I said. "I know how we can help Angie get well."

"Are you going to tell her doctor, or are you going to keep it a secret?" Wendy asked.

"I'm serious. We should give Angie something to *do*. Something to make her sit up and start living again."

"But what can Angie do?" Wendy asked.

"Oh, lots of things. She can . . . ." I looked around the room. "She can read that Wonder Woman comic book."

"I don't want to spoil your fun, girls," Mommy said, "but from what I've heard about Angie, even reading a comic book might be too much of a strain for her."

"We could read it to her," I said.

"You just might have something there, Jenna," Wendy said. "Only not a comic book. She can have my copy of *The Bionic Joke Book*."

I looked at Wendy. She's the last person I'd suspect of owning a joke book.

"It came in my Sunshine Box," she explained.

That gave me another idea. "Let's give her some other stuff, too, and turn this into a regular Sunshine Box."

98

Wendy considered it. "That's not a bad idea," she said. "Let's go tell Sam."

Sam said he'd contribute a bag of potato chips.

"Where'd you get potato chips?" I asked.

"I saved them from the time Angie and me went to the snack machine."

"Yuck," Wendy said. "Stale potato chips."

"They're better than some dumb joke book," Sam said, "She can't eat a joke book."

Wendy gripped the wheels at her side. She looked like she was ready to spin out of the room.

"Wait a minute, you guys," I said. "You're forgetting that Sunshine Boxes are *supposed* to be a little dumb."

Wendy relaxed her grip on the wheels. "What are you going to put in the box, Jenna?" she asked.

"I don't know. I'll have to think about it."

Back in my room, I tried to think of something to give Angie. But all I could think of was that small dark room.

When Mavis's mother heard what we were doing, she reached into her yellow tote bag and pulled out a kaleidoscope.

Mavis's lower lip trembled. "I thought everything in that bag was for me," she said.

"Don't worry, sweetheart." Mommy patted her hand. "Mommy will get another kaleidoscope just for Mavis."

Jim produced a cardboard box to hold everything, and everyone began to decorate it with crayons and paper cutouts.

Everyone, that is, but me. I still couldn't think of anything to give Angie, and I was beginning to panic.

I wanted to give her something special. Something that would make her sit up, turn on the lights, open the windows, and hang her broomstick legs over the side of the bed again. Something she would have given me back in her old days of being a busybody.

I thought about those days and knew at once what I would give her. I went over to my locker and found it there, ready to assemble.

"A kite!" Wendy cried when she saw what I had made. "We don't have room in the box for a kite!"

"I don't care. I'll give it to her separately."

Wendy sniffed. "Suit yourself."

19

We waited all afternoon and into the evening to see Angie, but Jim kept saying she was resting.

"Resting, resting, resting," I complained. "Why does she need so much rest?"

Nobody said anything.

Finally, in the morning, Jim said we could see her. Mommy decided the trip to Angie's room would be too tiring for Mavis, but Sam carried the kite while I pushed Wendy's wheelchair down the hall.

Mrs. Salvadore was standing at Angie's door, waiting for us, but I almost didn't recognize her. She had fresh lipstick and a big smile on her face.

"I'm so glad you could come," she said. She smiled and talked just the way Mother does when grownups come to our house.

She led us into the room. Somebody had pulled up the shades, which made everything look a lot brighter. The head of the bed had been raised, and Angie was propped up with two big white pillows.

Angie smiled at us, with her lips closed, the way kids with braces smile for their school pictures. We lined up at the foot of her bed and smiled back.

"So what's new?" she asked. Her voice sounded hoarse.

"We brought you a Sunshine Box," Sam said.

"You're kidding."

Sam held out the box, but Angie didn't even try to reach for it. Her mother took the box.

"What a beautiful box!" Mrs. Salvadore held it up so Angie could see the decorations on it. "We'll show it to Papa when he comes this weekend." Angie smiled, with her lips still closed.

Mrs. Salvadore opened the box and pulled out the joke book, the potato chips, and the kaleidoscope. She admired each item and asked Angie, "Isn't this nice?" Angie smiled and nodded.

I think we all realized it was a pretty chintzy Sunshine Box.

"Jenna didn't put anything in it," Wendy told Angie.

"That's because my present wouldn't fit." I walked out to the hall, where Sam had left the kite. I paused at the doorway for Angie to comment about how well I walked by myself, but she didn't say anything. I held out the kite.

"A kite. . . ." Mrs. Salvadore looked puzzled, and Angie's smile faded.

I started talking fast. "Remember, Angie, how you told me to put this together and make plans to fly it? Remember?" She nodded. "Well, I made it for you, Angie, because I want *you* to make plans to fly it."

Mrs. Salvadore looked away, but Angie stared at the kite.

"You forgot to put a tail on it," Sam said.

"It doesn't matter," Angie said, raising a hand to touch the kite. She looked at me and grinned with all her teeth.

Before we left, Mrs. Salvadore squeezed my shoulders and whispered, "We mustn't give up hope."

20

I'm going home.

I'm going to sleep in my own bed, eat in my own kitchen, sit in my own bathtub, and argue with my own sister. I'm even going to start junior high.

This is what I've wanted since the day I got here, so naturally I'm very happy. I think.

I don't know why, but every time I think about going home, I feel a little knot in my stomach. Maybe I'm catching something.

When I mentioned my knotty stomach to Wendy, she said, "You're just excited. And if you expect sympathy for that, you're crazy."

But Sam knew what I was talking about. He's going home tomorrow, too.

"I don't want to leave, either," he said.

"I didn't say I didn't want to leave. I just said my stomach feels funny."

"Then you've got one smart stomach," he said.

"Huh?"

"You know what happens after you go home?" He paused dramatically. "You go to *school*."

"School's not so bad."

"I'd rather stay here."

"With the nurses and their shots?" And I used to think this kid was smart.

"Everybody here thinks I'm the kid who knows the ropes," he said. "At school I'm just the sick kid."

"Aw, come on."

"It's true. Last year nobody wanted to play with me because I couldn't run or mess around. I had to be careful so I wouldn't hurt my head. Everybody thought I was weird."

"But that's all over with. Didn't the operation make your head better?"

"Yeah, but it also made me bald. Everybody's going to laugh when they see this dumb hat. Then somebody will pull it off, and they'll all go *yuck*."

I sighed. Little kids can be so cruel.

"You just wait and see," Sam said. "Kids'll probably laugh at your crutches and try to take them away from you."

"Don't be silly," I said. "They'll just look at them and . . . ."

And what? I thought about all those eyes, staring at my legs. No, they wouldn't stare. They'd probably sneak looks, the way Yoyo did.

But I don't want people sneaking looks at me like that. Just because I've got arthritis doesn't mean I'm a different person. I'm the same kid who finished sixth grade at Warner Elementary and spent the first half of the summer at the Cedar Ridge Pool.

No, that's not exactly true. I've changed, but not just because of the arthritis.

Suddenly I understood what Angie had been trying to tell me. Why she wanted me to make the kite, get rid of the afghan, say no to Celia's help.

She wanted me to be Jenna Matthews. Not the crippled kid.

But how do I do that? How do I fly a kite when I can't run to get it up in the air? How do I keep from being a crippled kid when my legs don't work right?

I didn't need to hear anything else from Sam. I needed to think things out. Better yet, I wanted to talk them out— with Angie.

Angie's been in and out of the hospital for a couple of years now. And all the time she's been getting skinnier and skinnier. When she's gone back to school, she's probably even passed out. But I bet nobody ever called her the sick kid. She wouldn't let them. How did she do it?

I knew she'd tell me because, if there's one thing Angie likes to do, it's give advice. I picked up my crutches and began the long walk to her room.

The door was closed. Angie must be feeling better if she's shutting hospital doors again.

I opened the door.

The shades were up, and sunlight poured over the crisply made bed. It was empty.

I stood there, I don't know how long, staring at that bed. Maybe they had moved Angie to another room, closer to the nurses' station. Yes, that was it. They'd moved her.

I turned to leave. Jim stood at the door, holding a red, white, and blue kite. I saw what his eyes were telling me, and I hated him.

"Get out of my way!" I yelled. "I've got to find Angie!"

He held me back, then half carried me over to the bed. He sat down beside me.

"I was just taking this down to your room" he said. "Mrs.

Salvadore said Angie would want you to have it." He placed the kite on my lap.

I looked at it and screamed.

I don't know how long I kept screaming. After a while it was like I stepped out of my body and could see this dumb girl sitting on a hospital bed, screaming her head off.

I saw Jim hold her tight for a few minutes. Then he tried to shake her. But still she screamed.

God, she hurt my ears.

Above the screaming, I heard footsteps in the hall. The footsteps had voices, and they talked about what to do with the screaming girl. She was disturbing the other patients. Somebody had to do something.

Somebody did. She burst into the room and shouted, "JENNA!"

The screaming stopped, and the crying began.

I was sobbing into a big white uniform that smelled like right before you get a shot. I looked up and saw Anderson's fleshy face, with tears running down the creases.

There we were, sitting on a hospital bed, holding each other and crying. If only Angie could see us.

Anderson opened the drawer to the bedside table and pulled out a box of tissues. She handed me one and took one for herself. We blew our noses.

"No matter how many times this happens," she was saying, "I never get used to it."

"Angie was just a kid," I said. "Kids aren't supposed to die."

Anderson looked at me in surprise. It was as if she'd forgotten who I was.

"Angela was terribly ill," she said.

"I still don't understand."

"Neither do I."

Wendy and Sam both cried when they heard about Angie.
Even Mommy and Mavis cried a little, and they didn't even
know Angie.

But I couldn't cry any more.

"I know how you feel, kid," Jim said. "Angie was a good
friend."

That's not how I feel at all.

Angie was a rotten friend.

Everytime I turned around, she was laying some of her
busybody advice on me. Wear your glasses, Jenna. Make a
kite, Jenna. Get rid of the afghan, Jenna. Paint the tip of
your cane white, Jenna. Don't let Celia help you too much,
Jenna.

I never once asked for her advice, but she poured it on me
anyway. Then the one time, the only time, I ever wanted
advice, she wouldn't give it to me.

She went and died on me.

I felt guilty right away. Angie didn't want to die, any more
than I want to have arthritis.

If she had a choice, she'd sit up and dangle her broomstick
legs over the edge of the bed. She'd be building kites, teasing
candy stripers, and tracking down candy machines.

But she didn't have a choice. And neither do I.

Maybe my legs will keep getting better and better until
the arthritis goes away forever. Or maybe they'll get bad
again, even worse than they were this time.

I just don't know.

I wonder if Angie knew she was going to die.

21

Dr. Boggs brought his troop in early Thursday morning. He probably wanted to get out of the way before Mother arrived.

"You've done very well, Jenna," he said.

"Thanks."

"I'll keep in touch with Dr. Cosley. Make sure you follow his advice."

"Okay."

"Good luck." He patted my shoulder, like we were old buddies. Then he nodded toward the door, and his troop began its retreat. As they filed out, most of them smiled and told me to take care of myself, say hello to my parents, and enjoy junior high.

I wondered if they knew about Angie. Or cared.

After they left, I got dressed in a red skirt and a white top. It was the first time I'd worn regular clothes in almost a month. It felt funny.

I packed my stuff and double-checked the bathroom, my locker, my secret hiding place, and even under the bed. Everything was packed. Everything but the red, white, and blue kite. It stood in the corner, where I'd left it after my last trip to Angie's room.

"You're going home today, aren't you?" Mavis asked. She made it sound like I'd killed somebody.

"Uh-huh."

"I wanna go home, too!" She started to cry.

That's all I needed. Angie was dead, I was going home crippled, and now this kid was crying. Mommy'd better get here pretty soon. I looked toward the door.

My eyes stopped on the kite. *I think you should put together that kite and start making plans to fly it . . . . Everybody needs something to look forward to.*

I looked back at Mavis.

"After I'm gone, you can move over to the window bed," I said.

She shook her head. "I wanna go home!"

"The kid who's been in this room the longest *always* gets to stay in the window bed. You can look outside and see when your mommy comes in the front door in the morning."

"I wanna go home," she said, this time more softly.

"Of course, it's a big responsibility to be in the window bed. When you get a new roommate, you have to tell her everything—how to turn on the TV, how to make the bed go up and down, even how to find the secret hiding place. It takes a big girl to handle all that."

Mavis started taking stuff out of her secret hiding place to get ready for the move.

I decided to finish some other busybody business.

Wendy was staring out her window, with her back to the door and her neck held stiffly by the white plaster cast.

"I'm going home today," I said.

"Good for you," she said, still staring out the window.

"I'll miss you."

She spun her chair around. "Oh, no, you won't! You'll be

too busy with your old friends. And junior high. Nobody ever remembers the kids in the hospital after they get home."

"I'll write."

"That's what they all say."

"And when you get out of here, you can come visit me for a weekend."

She hesitated. "I couldn't do that."

"Why not?"

"Your parents wouldn't want me." She turned her chair back to face the window. "It would be too much . . . trouble."

"You don't know my parents," I said. "They'd consider it an educational experience. They want us to learn to get along with all kinds of people." I paused. "Even crabby people."

I walked around Wendy's chair so I could see her face. Sure enough, she was smiling.

Out in the hall, a Pink Lady was pushing Sam in a wheelchair. He was wearing shorts and a yellow T-shirt. His Charlie Brown cap was pulled down low.

"Hey, Sam!" I said, and the Pink Lady stopped the chair. "I guess this is it," I said.

"Yeah." If turkeys could talk, they'd use that same tone of voice to describe Thanksgiving.

"Well, good luck." It seemed like we ought to do something. I put out my hand, and we shook.

"We really must be going," the Pink Lady said. "Sam's parents are waiting downstairs." She started to push his chair down the long corridor.

"Just a minute!" I called after them. The chair stopped. "Couldn't you hang around the office and find out what's happening at school?" I asked Sam.

Sam turned to look at me. "The office?" He shook his head. "No. But maybe the locker room."

The wheels were turning.

Back in my room, a nurse's aide was already stripping my bed. Mavis was filling my secret hiding place with her stuff. It looked like I'd never been there.

Mother and Daddy came in and hugged me.

"We just heard what happened to Angie," Mother said, "and we're so sorry."

She kept on hugging me for a long time, and Daddy put his arms around both of us. I felt something heavy crumble inside me, and I started to cry.

I just stood there, with their arms around me, crying. I don't know whether I was crying about Angie or me or what. I just cried. I didn't care what Mavis or anybody else thought.

Finally Daddy handed me his handkerchief, and I blew my nose.

"Are you ready to go?" he asked.

I nodded.

The same Pink Lady who'd taken Sam away brought a wheelchair for me. I said good-by to Mavis and sat down. Jim placed the kite across my lap and patted my shoulder, just like Dr. Boggs had.

As we started down the hall toward the elevators, Wendy called out, "Don't forget! I'm coming to visit you!"

Yoyo was waiting for us when we got off the elevator. "Surprise!" she shouted, jumping up and down. We didn't kiss, but she got real close, and we almost hugged.

"Look," I said. "I put together the kite you gave me. But it needs a tail."

"We can make one at home," she said. She started to say something else, but Daddy hustled her off. He said she had to help him find the car. I knew he wanted to tell her about Angie.

The Pink Lady, Mother, and I waited inside the glass doors, watching for the car.

"It's pretty windy out there," Mother said. "Maybe I'd better take your kite so it doesn't fly away."

"No, I'll hold it."

The car pulled up, and the Pink Lady pushed the wheelchair through the automatic doors. A gust of wind whipped through the breezeway. I held the kite tighter.

Daddy hopped out of the car and opened the door to the back seat. I stood up and reached for the door. Another gust of wind, and I saw the kite sailing with it.

"Get it!" I shouted.

Daddy raced after the kite through the breezeway. He followed it around the corner and out of sight.

In a few minutes he came back, with the kite under his arm and a triumphant grin on his face. "I got it!" he said. "I didn't think I would, but I got it!"

"Oh, goody!" Yoyo said. "I'll fly it for you when we get home."

"Don't you dare," I said, taking the kite from Daddy. "*I'm* going to fly it."

"Okay," she said. "I'll get it up in the air, and then you can hold the string."

I looked at her. She sure didn't look like Coach Thompson's champion. She just looked like a kid who wanted to be important. I thought of Sam.

"You can help with my exercises," I told her, "But I have to fly this kite by myself."

"But Jenna, you have to *run* to get a kite up in the air."

"Maybe I won't do it today," I said, "and maybe I'll need a souped-up wheelchair to do it, but I'm going to fly this kite all by myself."

Yoyo looked at me like she was trying to figure out what size strait jacket I should wear. But I knew Angie would be grinning. And maybe even squirting water through her teeth.